The Circus in the Woods

THE
Circus
IN THE
Woods

by Bill Littlefield

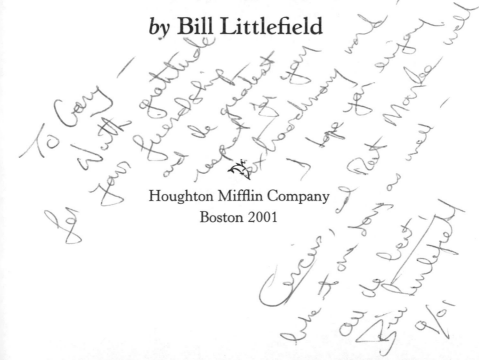

Houghton Mifflin Company
Boston 2001

Acknowledgments

Thanks to Ann Rider, a thoughtful and thorough editor, and to
Alison Kerr Miller, the book's copyeditor.

Thanks to Dr. Christopher Salvo for sharing his expertise on bee
stings and comas.

Thanks to Sandy Kaye, Charles Pierce, Conall Ryan, and to
various other friends/writers who reminded me from time to time
that I should be writing.

Thanks to everybody at Highland Lodge, especially Snow.

Thanks to Paula Cabral for administrative assistance.

Copyright © 2001 by Bill Littlefield

The poem on pages 110–11 and 182–83, "The Song of the Wandering Aengus" by William
Butler Yeats, was first published in 1899.

www.houghtonmifflinbooks.com

The text of this book is set in 11.5-point Horley Old Style MT.

Library of Congress Cataloging-in-Publication Data

Littlefield, Bill.
The circus in the woods / by Bill Littlefield.
p. cm.
Summary: Molly, her parents, and her sister spend most summer vacations at a camp in
the Vermont mountains, and as the years pass, Molly is led to find a mysterious circus
within the woods nearby.
ISBN 0-618-06642-X
[1. Vacations—Fiction. 2. Camps—Fiction. 3. Coming of age—Fiction.
4. Supernatural—Fiction. 5. Sisters—Fiction. 6. Vermont—Fiction.] I. Title.
PZ7.L73583 Ci 2001   [Fic]—dc21   2001016921

Manufactured in the United States of America
QUM   10 9 8 7 6 5 4 3 2 1

For Mary, Amy, and Alison, and for Mom,
who had this terrific suggestion about where we
might spend a couple of summer weeks

ONE

THERE WAS CERTAINTY IN THE SAMENESS OF EACH SUM-
mer. At least that was true when I was a child. Or for a time
it seemed to be.

Halfway through August we would pack the station
wagon with a week's worth of T-shirts, shorts, and books,
carrying loose in the back seat enough tapes to last the long
ride to Vermont. They were the same tapes each summer,
stories read by narrators with recognizable voices. Roald
Dahl was a favorite. Over time my sister, Kip, and I came to
know not only the words but the cadences of the narrators
by heart. We could have recited the worn stories to each
other, but each year we brought the tapes and played them,
and in the front seat our parents groaned.

The car never broke down, and we never had the excite-
ment of an accident. Mom and Dad were careful drivers,
and, though our house always looked lived-in and the yard
went its own way, they took care that the car was in good

running order before we took on six hours of driving. I remember that in that back seat, surrounded by our pillows, our puzzles, and our tapes, we felt safe. Sometimes, lulled by the sameness of what would come next, we'd sleep.

One year, toward the end of our week in Vermont, Kip and I woke up earlier than usual, too early for breakfast. (We shared a room when we were there, so when one was up, the other was.) My father was already sitting on the crooked porch of our cabin, looking down the hill to the pines. When he heard us, stumbling and sleepy, coming out of the bedroom, he leaned in from the porch and put his finger to his lips. He wanted us to let our mother sleep. Maybe that morning she did. When we'd pulled on our shorts, T-shirts, and sneakers, we padded out to the porch to be with him. Down the hill the shades of green ran into one another. Across the road below us we could see the path that led through the woods to the lake. My father stood up and beckoned, and we followed him.

The way down the hill was worn and easy. The early sun — it was probably six o'clock or a little after — hadn't dried the grass yet, and by the time we crossed the road and entered the woods, our sneakers were damp. It had rained for a week before we'd arrived, and the path was still muddy. (It always seemed to have rained before we got to the lodge, and sometimes we'd hear later that it had rained after we left.) At several points there were little sidetracks where guests had tried to find their own ways over ferns and fallen branches to avoid the mud.

The path came gently out of the woods into a small, neat clearing, at the far side of which we saw the gray boards of the weathered boathouse. Beyond the boathouse there was a narrow strip of sand that wound around the lake, except at the places where the trees came right down to the water. Sometimes you realized you were hearing the lake just before you saw it. It lapped against the sand and left a little froth, and on that morning, when nobody else had been down the path to the beach, we heard it first. In the afternoon, which was when almost everybody swam, there would be mothers and fathers on towels trying to keep one eye on their wet children, boys showing off how they could swim to the raft and push each other into the water and shout about it, girls pretending not to watch, or girls asking for the ten thousandth time if they could take out a paddleboat or a canoe by themselves and their eyes going wide with surprise when the answer came back yes for the first time.

But now, early in the morning, the lake was quiet and impossibly flat. The raked sand was cold on our feet, and we — Kip and I — felt like interlopers. Of course my father had known what he would find. He looked out over the mist that was still rising from the water. He listened to the sad and spooky call of the loon — a bird we'd learn to spot with time but couldn't find that morning — and he said, "It's beautiful, isn't it?"

Kip didn't hear him. She was looking for rocks and shells. She always found several hundred she wanted to keep, and she gave the best ones names. She loaded them into paper bags, which always ripped. Then at the end of the week there was always a battle about how many she could take home in the car.

"Of course," I said. "It always is."

What did he expect? We'd been here before. We always came in August. It was always beautiful.

TWO

WE DIDN'T ALWAYS WAKE UP EARLY, AND WE WEREN'T always the first ones to the lake. We *were* often the first ones to breakfast, which began at seven. It was served at the lodge itself, the main building — a place of not only breakfast and dinner, but Ping-Pong and other games; T-shirts with pictures of the lodge on them; tennis rackets that you could borrow; books that years and years' worth of guests had read and left behind on smooth, warped shelves; maple sugar candy; and a television nobody ever watched.

Breakfast was memorable, even to a child — probably even to Kip. In the kitchen they would make you chocolate chip pancakes, even if chocolate chip pancakes weren't on the menu. There were apple pancakes with walnuts, too, and peach pancakes, and blueberry pancakes, so you can see why you would remember them, even if you were too little to finish them, which Kip was. And she'd get blueberries all over her face. If we'd picked blueberries on the hill behind the lodge the day before, which we often had, there would be a card in the menu that said "Blueberries Picked by Kip and Molly." There was hot chocolate and there were homemade muffins of all sorts — apple, raspberry, bran (on unlucky days) — and blueberry coffee cake with a sugary top, and there was cereal for when you couldn't eat pancakes and muffins and coffee cake anymore, or when you didn't want to, because in Vermont you were always allowed.

In the morning we often ate on the porch, which was wide and white and ran the length of the front of the building, slanting away from the lodge itself. In some places it slanted a lot. It was quiet, even hushed, if you got to breakfast first, and always full of talk and the clink of spoons and dishes before very long. Some people planned their day at breakfast on the porch. We didn't have to. Until the summer when I found the circus in the woods, our plans were always the same. When we had finished eating breakfast, and sometimes before we had finished, because we couldn't wait, Kip and I would push our chairs from the table with a squeak — carefully, if we were sitting in one of the places that really went downhill — and then we'd run around the lodge to Snow.

I understand now that Snow was the reason our parents thought the lodge would be such fun in the first place — for them. There was no way they could have known what fun she'd be for us. And of course we didn't know, either. In fact, the first summer we went to the lodge, when I was eight and Kip was only five, we both thought it was going to be horrible. Before we left, when Mom and Dad were trying to tell us what a wonderful place it was and how we'd have at least as good a time there as we ever had had on any vacation, they mentioned that there was a sort of day camp each morning, run by somebody named Snow.

I thought, *What a goofy name. I wonder if her brothers and sisters are named Rain and Sleet . . . or maybe Sunshine.*

Kip thought, *No!* and she didn't keep her thoughts to herself, "Sort of day camp! I've been to day camp. I'm finished with day camp. I don't have to go to any more day camps!"

On the way to Vermont that first August, she worried about it, loudly. While we were still an hour or so away from the lodge, after we'd passed our twelfth or fourteenth herd of cows, Dad, who was driving, mentioned that he'd heard that the cows outnumbered the people in Vermont.

When we passed the next herd, Kip groaned. "More cows."

She did it with the next herd, too, and the one after that, and it was funny for a while, and then not so funny, but she kept at it. By the time we'd reached the lodge, she was probably convinced that we'd have to step over, under, or around cows to get to the bathroom to brush our teeth and that it would be the worst vacation we'd ever had.

Her first look at the cabin where we'd be staying convinced her of it. It was only a living room with a sink at one end and a hall alongside. At each end of the hall was a small bedroom. The hall floor had warped and settled so that you felt as if you were on a boat when you were walking from one end of the cabin to the other. In the bathroom there was a white tub that sat up on curved legs that had once been painted to look like feet with little toes, but the paint had chipped off. And it smelled funny, at least at first. It smelled like old sun and pine needles and endless afternoons. It smelled like no hurry and bathing suits hung on the porch railing to dry next to the two old rocking chairs, upon each of which there always seemed to be an open paperback book, spine up. It smelled like the sound of that slanted hall when you walked on those tired boards. Later I would work to memorize that smell, so I could call it back anywhere and feel Vermont. But on that first afternoon it was just different — a little exciting for that reason, but mostly just different.

Kip and I fought about who'd sleep in which bed and who had to use the bottom drawer of the bureau — the one that was hard to pull out — and then it was time to explore.

Our cabin stood in a ragged row of eight cabins, all pretty much the same. Ours was highest on the hill, and from our porch you could see the lodge a little below us, and then the black ribbon of the road we'd arrived on (after a couple of wrong turns) and the beginning of the path that ran into the woods on the other side of the road. This was the path that led to the lake, the path that was sometimes muddy. You could also see the lake itself, or at least a big part of it, though not the near shore, of course, which was obscured by the trees.

The lodge was two hundred years old and comfy. It looked

as if it had always been there and belonged just where it was. It looked as if George Washington could have tied up his horse out front, taken off his three-cornered hat, and clumped up the steps to see about a room. From our cabin you could see the porch on the left side of the lodge, the same porch that also ran around the front, where we sometimes ate our dinners, too, if it was still warm and not too windy and all the tables weren't already full.

On the first morning we were there, after breakfast (which was certainly pancakes, though I can't remember which kind) my father looked at his watch and said, "Time to go see about this play program."

"No!" Kip shouted. "It's day camp!"

She thought she'd settled this in the car. When Mom and Dad had reminded us that there would be a program for us in the morning, she'd burst into tears. "I want to be with YOU on our vacation," she'd cried. "I'm not going on vacation to go to day camp. I went to day camp at HOME!"

I'd stuck out my own tongue at the idea earlier, but when Mom and Dad had said we didn't have to go if we didn't like it, I'd shrugged and said okay. That was fair. What if the program had potato chips? What if there were Popsicles? It might be fun.

But Kip hadn't given up so easily.

"I hate it!" she said as we walked around the lodge to see what the program was all about.

Actually, we already knew a little. When we'd been exploring late the previous afternoon, we'd looked in all the windows of the playhouse. (We knew the little red wooden building behind the lodge was the playhouse, because it said PLAYHOUSE in big white letters over the door. Kip couldn't read that first summer, of course. She was only five. But I was almost nine, and I could.) There were all sorts of pictures on the walls, paintings and crayon drawings, and there were dolls and animals, balls of all sizes and colors, and in one corner what looked like a stack of board games, probably for rainy days. Along one wall was a long table covered with projects — buildings made of Popsicle sticks, branches decorated with ribbons, piles of shells and shiny stones . . . all sorts of things. In another corner leaned a big, old, unpainted wooden bookcase that looked like any moment it might fall down under the weight of all the books jammed into it. On one wall there was an old map, curling at its corners, and I wondered what it was a map of. There was a big, hand-lettered sign on another wall that said FRIENDS FOREVER. Even in the late afternoon, when no lights were on inside, you could see that it was a good place.

So as we walked around the lodge on that first morning, after our first breakfast, I was looking forward to what might come next. But not Kip.

"I hate it!" she said, more quietly this time.

"How do you know?" my dad asked her.

"Yeah, Kip," I said. "How do you know? Let's see what it's like."

For a moment she looked at me as if I'd betrayed her. Then she changed tactics.

"You'll stay here?" she asked Dad. Her lower lip was trembling.

"Absolutely," he said.

The three of us walked up the slope between the back of the lodge and the playhouse. The grass was still a little wet with dew. Already there were toys in the yard in front of the playhouse — a volleyball, a beach ball, two of those bright, plastic, three-wheel cycles — all looking ready for children in that morning sunshine, though the children, I thought, would have to be a little younger than I was. I hadn't played with a beach ball in a while, even at the beach.

Just before we reached the doorway of the playhouse, Snow came out to meet us. Now, I would describe her as country healthy. She was ruddy rather than tan, and she walked with a vigorous sort of sailor's roll, as if she were in step with the shifting and spinning of the planet itself, something she alone could feel but which she took for granted and enjoyed. She must have been older than she seemed, because she seemed like a big child: excited and enthusiastic but at the same time serene. Her hair was brown shot with gray, and, although she had tied it up in a loose bun, at nine in the morning it was already struggling to get free, and it was succeeding. Her eyes were blue, though it took me some time to be sure, because they were always moving and they sometimes seemed to change. She wore a bright, embroidered smock, a big square of lots of colors on white, jeans, and leather sandals. I thought her long toes must be cold in the wet grass.

11

Then, I would have described her as radiant, if I'd known the word, and so she seems to me now.

When she saw Kip's face, she slowed her gait so that we were walking toward each other at the same pace. At the moment for speaking, she said, "Good morning," and smiled. She did not say, "What's your name?" or "Aren't you a big girl?"

I did not love easily, even as a little girl, but I loved her right away.

Kip was less sure. She still had Dad's hand. He spoke first.

"This is Kip," he said, holding up her hand in his. "And this is Molly."

"Hello, Kip," Snow said. "Hello, Molly. I'm Snow."

She looked at me as she said my name, as if she knew that what she'd see in her first look at me would be very important. Then she smiled as if meeting somebody new was nothing but the great fun for which that morning had been made. What a big, welcoming woman she was!

"We're here for a week," said my father, for something to say.

"You're the first ones here this morning," Snow said to Kip. And then to me, "The treasure hunt's all ready. That's the first thing I do. But I could use some help setting up the crafts."

"Okay," I said, and off we went to the playhouse.

Kip waited a moment and then started after us. "Can I help, too?" she asked.

Snow stopped and turned back. She held out the hand I

hadn't taken. Kip ran to her side, and we walked up the wooden steps and into the playhouse. A few minutes later, my father appeared in the doorway. I was lettering signs that would show everybody where to look for crayons, Popsicle sticks, and glue. Kip was arranging long, thin strands of plastic — the stuff you weave into lanyards and fobs — by color. When she saw our father, she said, "We get to stay here until lunchtime, Dad. We'll see you then."

"Have a wonderful day," said Snow.

My father walked away. He looked back just once. Kip had already returned to arranging the craft materials. She was telling Snow about the cows we'd seen on the drive up the previous day. I was watching him go, and I waved.

THREE

ONCE OR TWICE DURING THE MORNINGS OF THAT FIRST visit to Vermont we saw Mom and Dad walking down the path to the tennis court.

Once Kip had to go back to the cabin for some shells she wanted Snow to see. "What were they doing?" I asked her when she thumped back into the playhouse.

"Reading," she said with a shrug. "They were sitting in the rocking chairs on the porch, just reading."

Who could understand them? If they'd asked, Snow probably would have let them decorate branches with bright bits of felt to make walking sticks. They probably could have come on our nature hikes. But they never asked.

On that first day, Kip and I had Snow to ourselves. After the scavenger hunt, we gathered around the map she had in the playhouse. Snow had marked all the paths through the woods at the lodge with different colored pencil lines. I picked the blue path — it was called the leopard path — and off we went.

Along the path, which was wide and easy, Snow showed us different plants and told us their names — Queen Anne's lace, jack-in-the-pulpit, fiddlehead fern. We saw the tracks of the deer that would sometimes come down to the lake early in the morning, and lots of smaller animals.

"What about leopards?" Kip asked.

"I haven't seen any leopards," Snow said. "Bears a couple of times, but not here. Way back in the woods."

"Elephants?"

I snorted, but Snow gave Kip her answer. "Not in Vermont," she said, "not unless the circus comes to Burlington."

Even on the mornings when it was just the two of us and Snow, the time passed more quickly than any time I've ever known. Snow always had a game or a hike or some other plan. We made pictures and collages out of scrap paper, wire, and beads. We tied and glued branches and scraps into little cabins or teepees. We made puppets with socks and put on plays. We kicked a soccer ball around the yard in front of the playhouse. And for the last twenty minutes before lunchtime, there were always stories.

Sometimes, the stories Snow read were the same ones Kip and I had heard at home — *Charlotte's Web* or *Stuart Little* or the poems in *Where the Sidewalk Ends*. Even then, when we knew the stories and Snow did, too, she could read each one as if we were finding just the old friend we should be happiest to encounter that day and not settling for something because it was available. She stopped a lot, too, to make the stories her own. In the middle of a chapter of *Stuart Little*, she'd close the book on her finger, look down the hill toward the game room, and begin to tell us about the time some children found a mouse there and chased it around the Ping-Pong table a couple of times and then out into the yard — not, thank goodness, into the dining room, where dinner was still being served.

"Did he wear a little vest and hat, like Stuart Little?" Kip wanted to know.

"No," said Snow. "And he didn't say anything, either. I don't suppose he could talk."

"And even though there's a lake here, I'm sure he didn't sail a boat on it," I said.

"No," Snow agreed. "I never saw him do that."

"Did they catch him?" Kip asked.

"No," Snow said. "He was like Stuart Little in that he could wriggle through spaces that looked much too small for him. He could squeeze himself under the screen door or disappear down a hole more quickly than you would think possible. They never caught him. And now I suppose he comes back only at night, when the game room is empty and anybody who'd even try to catch him has been asleep for a long time."

"So he's as smart as Stuart Little," Kip said.

"I guess he is!" said Snow. She could look at you as if

you'd said something so remarkable and so unexpected that in a hundred years nobody else would have ever thought of it. Then she'd open the book where her finger was and read some more about the Stuart Little in there.

Usually, of course, we didn't have Snow to ourselves. Lots of the families chose the Lodge precisely because Snow was there, and on a given day she might have four, or six, or ten children gathered around her: four-year-olds who clutched at her skirt and looked up at her with big, round eyes, astonished that anyone that big should have so much time and energy for them; seven-year-olds who jumped onto the plastic bikes and trikes she had and rode them, arms flailing, down the grassy hill by the playhouse; ten-year-olds who pretended to be too old for any activity Snow might think up, and who spent the mornings — or at least the first morning or two — struggling against her contagious enthusiasm before they gave in and had a good time despite themselves.

I don't remember it proudly, but, at some point after some summers had passed, I became one of those older children. Some days nobody could figure me out, least of all myself. I wouldn't know why, but I wouldn't want to give even Snow the satisfaction of coming up with something I'd find fun. Sometimes I felt all by myself just because I felt all by myself. On those days, I could keep a straight face while Dad or Mom tried to make me laugh. I could squirm away from a hug. I'd go off by myself and read, or, if I was tired of reading, I'd ask if we could go to the lake, even though everybody else was having a fine time making walking sticks or shell castles. Or I would look down Snow's long table littered with scraps of colored felt and puddles of white glue and see no magic at all, only a mess. I'd wonder how Snow could stand it. I'd worry that if I grew up any more, I'd just want to turn that cluttered table over and walk away. And once, on one of the few wet days we ever had during our Vermont summers, one of those days when you could not walk from the playhouse to the lodge without getting your sneakers so sandy and wet that they would have to dry on the cabin porch for a whole day, I just went.

Snow must have thought I'd gone back up to our cabin or that I'd seen Mom and Dad heading for the lodge and gone to join them. Mom and Dad would have thought I was still with Kip and Snow. I didn't know how late in the morning it was, so I didn't know how much time I had before I'd be missed. There was nothing planned about my excursion, but I suppose I knew that what I was doing was wrong. Otherwise I might have walked down the hill past the lodge and across the road, where I'd have picked up the path we used nearly every day to get to the lake. Even on that rainy day, half a dozen people would have seen me on that path before I entered the woods. Instead, I slipped around behind the playhouse and cut through the woods up the hill from the lodge. There were paths there, too, and dirt roads, but nobody used them in the summer. They were trails for the cross-country skiers. They didn't lead anywhere except back on themselves and around in loops.

At first I just enjoyed the pleasure of being by myself. I kicked at the leaves and stones in the path. I had a water bottle with me, so this walk in the woods must have been at least a half-shaped plan after all. I don't remember. It was a little dark and wet — my socks were damp in no time — and when I turned from the trail onto one of the dirt roads, the wet clay and sand stuck to my blue sneakers. I was walking uphill, but it was a pleasant exertion. There was nothing extraordinary to see, no spectacular view of the mountains on that gray day, and as I walked I noticed some of the flowers Snow had named for us. I didn't notice much else for some time — twenty minutes? forty? — until I came to a place where the dirt road was intersected by another path.

I'd stayed on the road so that whenever I decided I'd been alone long enough I could turn around and walk back to the playhouse or the lodge or our cabin as directly as I'd walked away. That only seemed good sense, and it was a kind of sense I had even on the days when Mom and Dad would roll their eyes and give up on me. But here was a path I'd never noticed before on our walks with Snow, and though you might think all paths in the woods must look pretty much alike and wonder why one should be noticed rather than another, this one, above most, should have been, because on a big oak tree at the start of it there was a crooked piece of wood shaped just a little like an arrow, and on the piece of wood somebody had written CIRCUS.

I never hesitated. That was strange, because I was not an especially brave child. It wasn't that I was a coward, either, but I was careful. I know that partly from memory, and partly because of what I've been told lots of times. In fact, I had been told so just a couple of mornings before my walk. I'd taken one of the trikes to the top of the hill where the playhouse sat and ridden it down toward the lodge. My mother was watching.

"You've outgrown that," she said, and laughed.

She was right. My knees were up around my chin.

"It's still fun," I told her.

"You wouldn't have done it when you fit on the trike," she said. "You'd have watched." Then she took a step toward me and leaned down to kiss me on the forehead. I let her. I wondered if any of the other kids were watching. It made me feel like a baby, but it wasn't an altogether disagreeable feeling.

The trail I was following was obvious and wide where it left the road, but it didn't stay that way. At a couple of forks I had to guess which path was the real trail, and once or twice I turned around to retrace my steps. Where the dirt road had been taking me gently up, the path seemed to be leading generally downward, and in a few spots it was so steep that I had to hold on to the trunks or exposed roots of trees to climb safely over the rocks. A lot of it was work, and soon my hands were dirty and my sneakers were covered with mud. There hadn't been a lot of people on this path. If it hadn't been for the CIRCUS sign where it started at the road, I'd have said that it was no proper path at all, only a channel that a flooded creek had found or a logging trail that had been out of use for so long that it had been forgotten.

Dirty, wet, and a little cold, I would have given up the adventure and turned back to find the road. But then I heard the music.

Once my father had told Kip and me of an annual school picnic he and his family had always gone to when he was my age and younger. The children gathered on a grassy hill that overlooked the playground behind the school he attended. (He showed me the school once on a trip to see my grandmother, so I didn't have to imagine the hill behind it. With his heavy briefcase, his cough in the morning, and his scratchy beard in the evening, it *was* impossible to imagine him as a little boy, though I had seen some pictures.) He remembered deviled eggs, which he did not eat, and popcorn, which an old man made in a noisy machine that sat on a two-wheeled cart in the black driveway at the top of the hill. He remembered how the boys chased the girls and the girls chased the boys, and how the children would roll down the hill, though they had been told not to, and how the night of the picnic was always warm and soft, and how, when he was a child, he didn't think that would ever change. But when he told us the story of the picnics, what he remembered most happily was the sound of the calliope that was always hooting and chirping on that evening. It stood next to the popcorn machine, patched and whistling, spewing steam. Its music, he said, was loud and antic. I'd heard a bagpipe once or twice, and when he would tell us the story of the picnics, I'd ask if the calliope was like that.

"Oh," my father would say, "a bagpipe times ten . . .

times a hundred. And less solemn . . . and no work for any-one, nothing for any man to blow on or wear himself out with. Just a big machine pumping loud and happy bleats of music into the twilight sky."

My father said that without the calliope, perhaps he wouldn't have remembered the picnics at all.

I had never heard a calliope. My father's best efforts to describe the sound of the wheezy old machine he remembered had been in vain. But when I heard the music in the woods, very faintly at first, I knew right away that a calliope was what I was hearing.

But that wasn't all I heard. Over the calliope, or somehow between the notes, there was laughing. It sounded like children.

Then I saw the dancer, and I'm sure that she saw me first. She was leaning out from behind one of the trees, as if she were too shy to welcome me but wanted me to come ahead. She was no bigger than I, but there the similarity between us ended. I was over my shoes in mud by then, and all scraped elbows and dirty knees from climbing down the disappearing trail. She wore a short pink dress with tights underneath, and white toe shoes. Her hair was a dark swirl, and I thought I could see freckles on her face. We were deep in the same woods, but there was no mud on her. She looked like she was ready for a recital, a cotillion. Or that was the impression she gave me in the moment she let me see her. Before I could reach the tree she'd leaned on or even call out for her, she was gone.

All along the trail, even as the going had become less certain and I'd had to guess and sometimes go back a bit and start again, I'd never been frightened. These were just the woods that surrounded the lodge — I'd walked through them with Kip and Snow so many times. I knew the names of the flowers. If I was not on one of Snow's trails now — we'd never seen the CIRCUS sign when we were in the woods together — or even if I was on no trail at all, I was still in the same woods. I could turn around any time I wanted to and find my way back. If that didn't work I could shout and a hiker working up an appetite for lunch would hear me and come get me or direct me back with a voice that I would recognize: one of the men who always played tennis before dinner, maybe, or the boy who raked the beach and put the canoes up in their racks when everyone had gone back to the lodge at the end of the afternoon.

But now the calliope was louder, or I was closer to it, and I didn't know if I'd be able to hear a voice calling me. When I looked up the hill I'd just climbed and half-skidded down, it was just a hill, not a hill parted by a trail. Halfway up it the trees seemed to have leaned together, and I couldn't see the top at all, though I must have come over it just a few minutes before. So I was frightened then — about as frightened as I was curious, or maybe a little more.

The calliope my father had described had been cheerful. Maybe the one I was hearing would have been cheerful, too, if the trees overhead hadn't blocked what sun there was. Or maybe it was the clouds. Here the trees were so thick that I couldn't tell what the weather was back at the lodge. Maybe it had turned into a beautiful day for the beach. Maybe the rest of my family was packing cheese sandwiches and apples and potato chips and cookies for a picnic, wondering where I was and whether I'd ruin the afternoon by being late. I wondered if enough time had passed for them to be worrying instead of just wondering.

The music didn't stop abruptly, or at least that's not how I remember it stopping. When it began — or when I first heard it — the music could have been a birdcall. It had become louder and more distinct as I walked, until it was a calliope. Now, as I looked up into the canopy of trees that blocked what sun there might have been, I heard birds. A crow first, insistent and loud. Then a handful of those little birds you hear in the morning — the ones whose three-note songs repeat and repeat, convincing people that the birds are happy that it's time to get up.

Even then I thought to myself, *If I tell Kip this part of the story, she'll say, "You fell asleep. You were dreaming and the birds woke you up."* Anybody would say it. Or anybody as sensible as a child. But though the woods were just the woods now, moss and wild grass underfoot and that almost impenetrable tangle of leaves and branches overhead, and the birds were just birds, I knew I hadn't been dreaming. I'd heard the calliope and I'd seen the dancer with the dark hair. Hadn't I been close enough to see her smile, too? And maybe hear her laugh? And the odd thing about that moment in the morning woods was that even then, when I was wet and dirty

24

and alone, as lost as I could be in a place I was sure, despite the evidence of my senses, that I knew, I was sure that it wasn't my sister whom I wanted to tell what had happened. It wasn't my mom, though I'd called for her often enough at night and she'd always come. It wasn't my dad, who'd have said 'Your eyes are so serious,' or tried to make a joke, which could make me almost mad enough to cry. It was Snow.

FOUR

W HAT I DID THAT MORNING WHEN I WAS HEARING THE
birds instead of the calliope was try to figure out where I
might be in relation to the lake. Even on the days you didn't
go there, the lake had the feel of being the center of things.
Way up on the hill, the lodge gave anybody rocking on
the porch the goofy illusion that she owned all that water.
There wouldn't have been much point to the rocking if you
couldn't see it. The road leading into town had signs pointing where you could turn off for the docks and landings.
Everything had grown up around the lake.

I was not on any path I knew, but I'd crossed the same
paths and at least one road that we'd crossed lots of times. I
couldn't have said whether I'd been walking east or west, but
I knew that, after a time, I'd begun walking downhill. Nothing was further down any hill across the road than the lake.

If that wasn't chapter two out of *The Woodsman's Guide*,
it was at least an idea. Without an idea, you were lost. (Of

course, I was lost in any case, but I was trying to keep that off to one side of my thoughts, in the same neighborhood as how wet and dirty I was and how hungry I was getting.)

I picked my way through more forest that didn't look as if it had ever known a path, still heading vaguely downhill. At some point I was sure to cross the dirt road that ran around the lake, wasn't I? Or at least a path that looked as if it might lead somewhere other than further into the woods? Briars caught my legs and the sunlight disappeared almost entirely a time or two, but finally I did come across a path. I didn't recognize it, but it had a friendly feel. I took the direction that seemed more likely to lead me down, still thinking that once I found the lake I'd be able to figure out where I was from there or find someone who could do that for me.

Before long there were blueberry bushes along the sides of the path and, after I'd walked past them, a patch along the way where the sunlight came powerfully through the trees that had been so thick.

These were good signs, I thought: blueberries I could eat if I got any hungrier — I did, and they were juicy and sweet — and sunlight to encourage me that, whatever else there might be to worry about, darkness, at least, was a long way off.

I began to walk a little more quickly. The path seemed to have leveled out, and I was almost sure that around the next turn in it, maybe just beyond a big oak tree that I could see now — one that bent to the left almost over the path, as if somebody had swung from it and bent it a hundred years ago

and it had never afterward been inclined to stand straight —
I would see the lake. I would come out of the woods to the
narrow beach, and somebody would look up from a lawn
chair or a towel he was sitting on and say, "Hello. Where
have you come from? You're just in time for lunch."

Or maybe it would be a part of the lake I didn't know. It
was a big lake. But there would be a fisherman there, just
packing up his line. "The lodge?" he'd say. "Sure. Come on.
Hop in the truck. I'll drop you there. How'd you end up way
over on this side?"

I fooled myself this way around several oak trees, across a
little brook that couldn't have helped but lead to the lake,
through a circle of mushrooms that a more superstitious
child might have worried about, and into a field of ferns. I
ate more blueberries, and two or three times I saw clearings
in the woods that looked as if the paths I could imagine beyond them would open to the beach. My sunbather and my
fisherman were joined by a young man who had just finished
repairing a hole in his canoe and offered to paddle me across
the lake to the lodge dock, and an old woman who'd become
lost herself, somehow, but who was sure that together we'd
have no trouble finding the path that would have us home by
lunch. Or dinner. Or breakfast at the very latest, which
would be all right, too, as she had a tent and sleeping bags.

When I was much younger — when Kip was no more than
three or four — my mother had taken us to visit a neighbor
who had a cabin in New Hampshire. The place was excep-

tional chiefly because this neighbor, who was over eighty, had been spending her summers in the cabin for almost all of those eighty-odd years and its living room bore witness to each one of them. There were dolls, little model trains, picture books, and glass animals of every description. They crowded one another off the mantelpiece and a dozen tabletops. It rained during the second day we were there, and Kip and I walked among the various treasures, to our mother's growing irritation. When the sun finally came out, our neighbor whose name was Helen and who was less afraid that we might break something than she was that Mom would break us, asked if we wanted to walk to Maine.

"Walk to Maine?" I asked. Maine was another state. It must be hours away, at least. Maybe we'd be gone all after noon. Could we pack a snack?

Behind thick glasses, Helen smiled and said that wouldn't be necessary. We followed her out the cabin door and down the stone steps into her yard. A rutted dirt road, muddy and dusty at once after the rain, ran in front of her place. Helen wore brown rubber shoes no higher than sneakers. They were two colors of brown, dark on the tops and light as caramel around the edges of the soles, which were rippled and thick. I remember them, because as soon as I saw them I wanted some.

"Follow me," she said, leading us up the road in the opposite direction from which we'd arrived the previous day. Kip started to sing: something tuneless and eternal and just right for a long march. But about a hundred yards along the road,

Helen stopped and took a few steps into the woods. She put her right foot up on a stone wall, which was really no more than a little row of rocks about eighteen inches high, and shouted, "Who wants to be first into Maine?" We took turns straddling the little wall, each of us standing for a moment in two states at once. Helen smiled at the surprise she'd provided. Then we went back to her cabin for tea.

I was that surprised when I stepped out of the woods in Vermont that afternoon when I'd first seen the circus. I don't think a big sign saying WELCOME TO MAINE could have surprised me more. Maybe if the sign had said WELCOME TO WYOMING.

Because after all the walking I'd done along paths I didn't know and, before that, along no paths at all, always sure that I was aiming for the lake, here I was at the edge of a clearing where there was no beach, no young man at work on his canoe, no indolent sunbather looking up curiously at a bedraggled girl coming out of the woods from an odd direction. Here there was no wizard, either, with a long white beard and blue robe covered with stars. No sinister magician pointing the way with bony finger, smiling an inscrutable smile.

Here, instead, was our cabin.

Here, more precisely, was Kip. She was sitting with her back against a tree with one knee bent. She'd clipped the end of a twist of gimp to the shoelace of one of her sneakers, and she was working away at the other end of it, making a lanyard, maybe, or a necklace. She wasn't twenty yards from the cabin we had for those two weeks. The sun was still bright on the cabin porch, and I remember saying to myself, *That's why Kip's under the tree instead of in one of the wooden porch chairs.*

What I should have been saying to myself is *How the heck did I get here?*

What Kip said was "Boy, are you gonna get it."

I looked past her to the dirt road, which still ran down the hill. Around a bend to the left, about a hundred yards below the cabin, it would still run alongside the lodge itself. Across the paved road in front of the lodge, it would still become a path that got steeper as it crossed the grassy field where there might be ticks, "so stay on the path as I've told you a thousand times." Once it entered the woods, it would still be muddy if it had rained and just trampled grass if it hadn't. It would still cross the stream by means of a plank bridge that would sink toward the water as you walked over it and bounce you a little like a diving board if you jumped at just the right place in the middle. Through a little clearing it would still enter the woods again and then come out alongside the old, gray boathouse with no boats in it but only high shelves along one wall, upon which were stacked piles of gray sails that nobody had raised or lowered for a long time. Just on the other side of that boathouse would be the small and completely familiar beach, where the greatest possible surprise might be that the lodge had acquired a new paddleboat, which somebody had painted bright blue.

I knew all this as surely as I knew my name. And I knew with the same certainty that for the longest stretch of the afternoon, I had been walking down rather than up, toward the lake rather than away from it, looking for a landmark or a helpful stranger who might point me home.

"I said, you're gonna get it," Kip said, more loudly this time, and, I thought, more hopefully.

As it turned out, she was disappointed. Mom had begun to worry only just before I showed up, and Dad wasn't concerned even then. Or Kip said he said he wasn't. She'd been listening from her spot below our cabin's porch when Mom had come out to see if Dad knew where I was.

"I haven't seen her for hours," she said.

"I'm sure she's all right. She's probably gone to the desk to see if there are more families with kids coming in today. Or maybe they recruited her for blueberry picking, or she's helping Snow set up for tomorrow. She's as much a helper as a camper this summer."

"More," my mother had argued, according to Kip, and this is where the conversation had turned alarming, from her point of view. Because next my mother said, "I don't know how much longer it will make sense to come back. Molly's almost too old for Snow's camp now. We don't want to push it so that she's moping around and complaining about not wanting to hang around with the little kids."

After Kip had repeated this much of the conversation for me, I could have come up with the rest of it. Dad would have said that I *liked* being a helper with the littler kids. Mom would have told him yes, sure, but it would be better if I was palling around with kids my own age. Dad would have

32

shrugged and said there was plenty of time for that and, besides, this was just two weeks out of the summer. Mom would have sighed, smiled, and said, "I don't think you want her to grow up." Dad, depending on the mood he was in, would have protested or agreed. Once Mom had told me that he'd been sad for days after my first tooth came in. I loved that story, at least on the days when I wasn't feeling that I couldn't wait to grow up: days when I walked off into the woods by myself.

But on that afternoon, Kip had interrupted the conversation before it could get to "I don't think you want her to grow up." At the first hint that this might be our last, our next-to-last, or even our next-to-last-but-one summer vacation at the lodge, she'd jumped up from her place in the shade and told Mom and Dad that she wanted to keep coming back forever.

"And Mom laughed," Kip told me later. "I wasn't trying to be funny. She said, 'Forever's a long time, sweetheart.'"

I could hear my parents' voices as Kip recreated their discussion. (They'd have called it a discussion if Kip had told them to stop arguing, which she always did.) I even knew where the conversation would have gone next. My father loved the two weeks at the lodge. He liked to plunk down in the cabin, unpack everything, and call the place home until it was time to gather all the stuff together again, cram it into the station wagon, pop one of the familiar tapes into the cassette player,s and go home. He sometimes grumbled about how long it took for dinner to arrive and how fidgety Kip or

I might get at the table, but there were usually half a dozen kids in the dining room, some of them more restless than we were. The parents could shrug at each other and release us, and we could rush off together to play Ping-Pong or throw water balloons at one another while all the adults pretended to be more exasperated than they were. Then one of them would call from the porch, and we'd all run back for dessert.

My Dad thought Snow's camp was the best idea anybody had ever had. It left him and Mom with three hours free, even if Kip couldn't understand how anybody could sit still that long. Sometimes Dad and Mom would meet another couple whose kids Kip and I would play with, and they would hike together or play doubles on the clay tennis court that mostly just sat empty in the sun. Usually, by the time we came back to the cabin after camp, Dad would be back on the porch. He liked to see us coming.

"How'd it go?" he would ask Kip.

"Good," she'd say, and she'd rush ahead to show him whatever she'd made that morning out of sticks or string.

FIVE

THERE WAS A PICTURE AT SOME POINT— MAYBE IT'S STILL in an album packed away in a box somewhere — of Kip and me coming back up the hill to that cabin for lunch. Kip is running ahead. I don't remember whether we're carrying art or crafts or little seedlings in cardboard pots. Almost certainly we're carrying something. The ground is covered with pine needles and the sun is bright on the trail itself and on us. To get that picture, Dad must have been waiting for us. He must have looked at his watch, put down his book, gone inside for the camera, and then walked out to the trail to find a spot where he could see us come around the bend in the path. He must have had in mind our coming home.

I wonder if the picture is the image he thought of when he hauled himself off the porch and walked over the creaky boards for the camera? I wonder if he wanted not only to catch us coming up the hill, but to stop us, too, to make us pose? We wouldn't stop any more than a fast train would pause at a cardboard sign. He must have known it. Everybody does. Even I was beginning to learn it. But the signs litter the tracks.

Whatever Dad had been after with that picture, the result was close enough that he chose it for an album, but there were hundreds and hundreds of pictures in a whole shelf of albums. I remember two identical leather binders, one labeled "Molly: 0–6 months" and the other "Molly: 6 months to 1 year." In the first there are pictures of Mom, pregnant. In my favorite she is standing, big-bellied, on one leg, her arms stretched out as if she's dancing. The sun is behind her, as it would later sit behind Kip and me as we came up the trail. Her blond hair shines. There are woods around her, and, for once, she is out-goofing my dad. She is indescribably beautiful and silly. On one leg, she is dancing the dance of the woman who can dance if she wants to, a dance that says, "Don't give up your chair for me. I'm fine. Because pretty soon I'm gonna have the world's most amazing dancing baby, dancing before she's born."

The albums are full of lots of pictures of Kip, too, but the picture-taking apparently slowed down after I was a year old. The images are more thoughtfully chosen, like the one of Kip and me on the trail on the way to the cabin after Snow's camp.

We didn't come back the next summer. Instead, we traveled, because my Mom thought that if we didn't do it then we never would. Kip, who overheard so much, told me that.

"She said pretty soon you wouldn't want to go anywhere with the whole family. Not even to dinner or a movie. She said you were going to grow up."

I was braiding her hair, which was long but about to be cut short because Mom said Arizona would be hot, we'd be moving from national park to national park, and there might not be time every day for washing and braiding long hair.

This growing up didn't come as a revelation. Mom and Dad had joked about it when they bought me new shoes that Mom almost could have worn. I could drive her nuts in about a minute and a half by taking a shirt out of her drawer, holding it in front of me, and asking her if I could wear it to school. When we read together at night, there was less room on the big bed where my parents slept. Some nights it seemed as if every time I moved I'd kick Kip in the back or whack her with my elbow, and Mom and Dad both said that when I walked, I stomped.

"Ow!" Kip said. I guess I'd pulled too tightly at her hair. "Are you gonna grow up? We won't have as much fun in Arizona as we do in Vermont, will we?"

"Sorry," I said.

"I'll miss Snow," she said. Sometimes Kip couldn't talk and listen on the same day. "And I'll miss chocolate chip pancakes on the porch. I'll miss Heather and Lydia and the other kids we meet there sometimes. I'll miss the kids we'll never meet, because they'll be with Snow while we're in stupid Arizona."

"Heather and Lydia are going to Europe with their parents this summer," I said.

"I'll miss them anyway," said Kip.

I tied off the braid I'd been working on with a rubber band and started on the other one. Kip's hair was two shades lighter than mine, we'd decided. Our eyes were the same brown.

"I'll miss the paddleboats," Kip said.

"Maybe there will be paddleboats in Arizona. In one of the brochures Mom has, there's a lake."

"There won't be Snow," Kip said.

"Not in Arizona in the summertime," I said. It was a time when I was beginning to understand how easily my family could fall into my sarcasm trap.

"No, I mean we won't see Snow this summer. She'll be in Vermont, and we'll be in stupid Arizona."

I knew Kip would have a great time in Arizona. Kip had a great time wherever she was. She'd whine about not wanting to go and carry on about what a stupid place it was until we got there. Then, at the end of the trip, probably as we were sitting in the airport waiting to fly home, she'd say she wanted to come back next year.

But of course she was right about Snow. Kip went on complaining. I stopped listening. I felt like a traitor. I hadn't thought about Snow at all. Over the summers at the lodge she'd been a playmate, a big sister, a teacher, a guide — but she was more than that and especially important to us because she was ours, and one of us more entirely than anyone else was. She was like a babysitter who didn't have to report when the parents came home.

We didn't need Snow in Arizona. From reading, I learned

the word *antithesis* about the time we went to Arizona. Arizona was the antithesis of Vermont. It wasn't just hot where Vermont was cool. It was sun that started early, quit late, and would turn you red and sore anywhere you missed with the sunscreen. Sometimes in Vermont the day would begin so cold that we'd wear sweatsuits down to breakfast. We wouldn't get down to shorts and T-shirts until after the first hour with Snow. In Arizona, at least before we got out of Phoenix and into the mountains, the nights were so hot that when we came back to the hotel after going to a movie, Kip grumbled that they should have air-conditioned the parking lot.

But there was a difference bigger than that. Vermont was always "What did you make today?" "Let's see how far around the lake this path goes," or "Why don't we ask in the kitchen if they'll need blueberries in the morning, and we can pick some and get our names on the menu?" We all made it up as we went along. The Grand Canyon was grand, all right, about as spectacular as a hole in the ground could be, but you can't climb down into it any time you like. Before we'd get ten feet on the trail, a guy in a ranger's hat would stop us to make sure we were carrying water. He had already warned us about all the times they'd had to rescue people who thought they were going to hustle down to the Colorado River at the bottom of the canyon and then be back on the rim for lunch.

"Were their tongues hanging out?" Kip asked him. The ranger didn't even smile.

One morning we rode in a hot air balloon. We got up while it was still dark because it said in one of the ten thousand brochures Mom had that once the air *outside* got hot they couldn't get the balloon up. The balloon guy picked us up in front of the hotel in a fancy, air-conditioned sort of car/sort of bus. The balloon was folded up on a trailer behind us. We drove out into the desert, still only about half awake, and then stood watching as the balloon guy and his two helpers, who'd driven out there in the dark desert to meet us, hauled and tugged at the balloon, which is about as mobile as a circus tent when it's on the ground.

One of the helpers had a thick, gray mustache and wore a white cowboy hat and black, tooled leather boots. He was Arizona all the way. He could have been in the movies as the sheriff who should have retired before his hand began to quiver. The other helper, who I'm pretty sure was an Indian, had on a pair of new sneakers and a faded blue T-shirt with two jumping basketball players on it. Across the back of the shirt it said FOUR STATES SHOOTOUT, 1993.

Out of the truck the cowboy and the Indian pulled a machine that looked like a big canon. The cowboy fussed around under the machine for a while, and then suddenly it gave out a big *whoosh* and began filling the balloon with hot air. It was so noisy that if anybody else had been crazy enough to be out there in the desert before sunrise we'd have woken him up.

Sometimes you think you know how something will be, and then it isn't that way at all. I'd imagined that once you leave the ground in a balloon, there is no noise. You just drift away from the earth silently, lazily, pretty much heading just up. But what you really do is kind of clunk along over the desert for a little while as the balloon guy makes adjustments and shoots more hot air into the balloon, which makes about as much noise as Niagara Falls. The basket you're in bobs and pitches while your balloon decides whether it wants to go up at all, and you find yourself wondering if the whole balloon ride deal isn't a trick on tourists.

(Which reminds me, you feel like a tourist a lot in Arizona, no matter where you're from, because you've seen pictures on calendars and postcards of everywhere you're visiting, and everybody's selling Grand Canyon ashtrays and key chains and T-shirts. They sell T-shirts at the lodge in Vermont, too, but they're prettier and there aren't racks and racks of all the same ones.)

But we were up in a balloon. Because, after scraping along the ground a little, scattering stones in the red dirt as you go, you do finally get up in the air. The burner that heats the air and the fan or whatever it is that whooshes the air up into the balloon still make the same noise when you're up there, but you stop putting your hands over your ears when it happens. At some point you look down and see that you're not skimming the tops of the scrubby desert bushes anymore. You're sailing along a hundred and then two hundred and then three hundred feet above the ground, pointing as the occasional jackrabbit bolts and heads for some cover only he can find.

After a while we came up on some cliffs that had seemed a long way off. The balloon guy, whose name was David Windwalker (though I don't like to say it, because you won't believe that name, and maybe you won't believe anything else I've said or might say next, but it really was his name) pointed down at some cave openings. They were the dark spots against the stone, which the sun was already beginning to turn red.

"They found some pottery fragments in there," he shouted over the noise of the blower. Then, when the blower was off for a few minutes, he went on in a normal, deep voice. "There are some cave paintings, too, and nobody will ever mess up the ones in there, unless they can climb like goats."

I'm sure he was right. Looking at those caves from the balloon, you couldn't figure out how anybody'd get to them from below, which I guess was the point if you were living in the desert a few thousand years ago and didn't know what might be big and hungry and agile enough to try to find you some night as you slept, and then wake you with a roar, a screech, or a crunch.

David Windwalker — I know, that name again — told us that we were lucky, because not everybody who took his balloon ride got to see those caves.

"You mean you don't always go to the same desert?" Kip asked.

"Same desert," he said, "but different directions. It's the

wind that takes us where it wants to take us, once we get up here."

"Does it tell us how to get back where we started?" Kip may have been wondering if we were going to pull a Dorothy and end up somewhere other than Arizona.

David Windwalker smiled. Out of the inside pocket of his jacket he pulled a walkie-talkie. It was no bigger than a cell phone. He flipped a switch and said, "Have you got us?"

Clear and strong, the voice of the guy who looked as if he could have been a sheriff came back. "We got you, chief."

"Now," said David Windwalker to Kip, "look way off to the southeast where I'm pointing. You see that dirt road?"

Kip looked where he was pointing and said she did, but I couldn't see any road, and I don't think she could, either.

"You keep following along that road to where it disappears behind the beginning of that hill. In just a little while, you're gonna see something moving there, and dust behind it. That'll be the truck."

Then he talked into the walkie-talkie again. "Jack, you were right," he said. "We'll see you along the thirteenth fairway. Probably twenty minutes."

"Yeah, okay," the voice came back. "Keep your head down."

Mr. Windwalker clicked off the walkie-talkie and tucked it back into his jacket.

"Stray golf balls?" asked my Dad.

Mr. Windwalker smiled. Politely, I thought. "No," he

said. "This wind we're in today takes us over an old guy's farm. He says we scare his dogs, and they start barking and wake up his wife. Says if we don't fly somewhere else, one morning he's gonna shoot us out of the sky."

Kip grabbed Mom's hand, but I didn't believe it. Nobody takes tourists where somebody might shoot at them. As far as the "thirteenth fairway" was concerned, I thought that was probably balloon-guy code for something. There was no golf course in sight, even from several hundred feet. It was just desert and more desert, and what looked like a low ridge when Mr. Windwalker had pointed to the road beside it, but which was looking like a higher ridge little by little as we sailed lazily toward it. We were too high to see the jackrabbits Mr. Windwalker had pointed out earlier, but not high enough to see over the ridge. When we got closer to it, Mr. Windwalker gave the balloon another noisy blast of hot air so we'd clear the top with plenty to spare, and beyond the ridge the land looked as weird to us as Oz must have looked to Dorothy when she saw that that's where she was going to come down.

Lying flat and green and looking very small against all that desert was a patch of shiny lawn. The edges of it were straight, as sharp as if some giant had cut a square of green velvet from a mile-long bolt and staked it to the Arizona ground. Around one corner of the course there was an arrangement of little houses, which, even from the sky, you could see were not really so little. They were painted in different colors, all pastel. They looked like complicated shells that had been set along what would have been the world's straightest shoreline if the golf course had been the sea.

"Wow," Mom said.

"Yeah," said Mr. Windwalker. Then he said, "Hey," and he pointed again. I followed the line of his finger and, just where he said it would be, there was a thin cloud of red dust. The truck was churning along in front of it, looking like the piece you might buy if you were trying to finish off an impossibly great electric train set after you'd already bought all the trains.

"When they get this course finished and sell these houses, we'll have to find somewhere else to run this ride," Mr. Windwalker said.

Sure enough, by then we were going down. It was quieter than it had been on the way up. There was no need to blast hot air up into the balloon. Mr. Windwalker could tug on some ropes to kind of aim the balloon where he wanted it to be, but a sudden gust of wind could have dumped us on the clipped, green grass of one of the golf course fairways, and that could have been bad for business.

On the way back to our hotel in the truck, Mr. Windwalker told us that it used to be a tradition for balloonists to carry a bottle of champagne or wine among their supplies, because they'd found that farmers whom they'd startled with emergency landings — especially farmers carrying pitchforks or shotguns — were more reasonable if the balloonist landed bearing gifts. But building a golf course in the desert was serious business, he said, and a bottle of champagne wouldn't count for much if a cranky breeze dropped his basket on one of the greens and then dragged it over that silky carpet, tearing up the desert's only grass as its wicker bottom bounced along the turf.

Arizona was, as Mom and Dad hoped it would be, a great vacation. But after those summers at the lodge in Vermont, it was a kind of a vacation where there was too much moving too fast. It wasn't just that we went to three national parks in eight days, flying across the desert highways in our new-smelling, air-conditioned, just-like-everybody-else's rental car to reach them. It wasn't just that instant green golf course with its pink, yellow, and pale blue houses against the lonely desert, either, and it wasn't just visitors, like the developers or like us.

One day we went for a jeep ride on some roads that ran right up the steep red Arizona rocks and around curves that looked as if they'd tip the jeep on its roof or buck it off the hill and into a ditch. From time to time, the driver would stop somewhere and point out a rock formation on a distant mountain face. "That's the old witch of the mountain," he'd drawl. "See how her nose comes down all crooked and almost touches her bony chin where it's jutting out? And over there to her left and down just a little bit, that's her stable full of broomsticks. See 'em stickin' up in all different directions? All different sizes? She can slide down there a little after it gets dark, pick out the one she wants, and ride off to wherever she needs to go."

Maybe he should have been content with that kind of story. I guess I thought he should have. But on the way down the trail that would take us back out to the state road, he suddenly braked the jeep, threw it into reverse, and shouted, "Hold everything! I think I saw a deer!"

Wheels spinning and squealing, we backed furiously though the red dust, kicking loose rocks every which way. At the opening to a clearing I hadn't even noticed when we passed it coming down, he jumped on the brakes again. There would be no deer, of course. Deer were for Vermont, not the desert, and even if somebody'd dropped one among the red rocks by balloon, the shouting and the jeep and the flying stones would have scared it off. But we were tourists, so we all looked, behaving just as the driver knew we would.

"Sure enough," he said with a grin. At the back of the clearing was a little John Deere tractor, bright yellow, looking as if somebody would be back to crank it up any minute. It was just a cowboy jeep driver's joke, harmless, unless you let yourself think about what the heck the tractor was going to be doing out there among those rocks that nobody'd bothered in a couple million years.

And that tractor wasn't the only sign. My dad had bought new sneakers for the trip — something he wouldn't have done for Vermont — and he got a blister. One morning in Sedona, after breakfast in a restaurant that had one hundred different kinds of pancakes (but none of them as good as any at the lodge), he set off in search of Band-Aids. An hour later, while Kip and I were still fighting about who'd left the wet bathing suit on the bed the night before, he came back and dropped into a chair in the little living room of the condo where we were staying that night. Mom was looking at a map at the table in the kitchenette, because at nine-thirty in the morning it was already too hot to sit on the little porch out front, which never would have happened in Vermont.

"Any luck?" she asked.

"You can buy all the postcards you'll ever need here," Dad said. "T-shirts and Indian jewelry, too, and jewelry that looks as if it might have been made by people only pretending to be Indians, or by Indians who didn't care anymore. You can buy angels in almost every store. I don't know what it is about this town and angels, but you won't find more of them for sale anywhere: cute ones, of course, cheruby little characters with long lashes and their eyes closed, but high-end angels, too, worked in metal or carved out of cedar. Prisms are also popular. Also, pictures purporting to show auras, whatever they are, and guidebooks with maps indicating the best routes to the vortices."

"The what?" Mom asked.

"We are among the vortices," Dad said. "Almost every hill in the neighborhood has a vortex on top. It's supposed to be where an energy center occurs. You can be restored and renewed, physically and spiritually, just by standing in the right place and feeling the vibes. It's wise to get there early, especially if you're aiming for a vortex that doesn't require much of a climb. The people who need restoration and renewal form a long line. They've all bought the same maps.

You can find the maps anywhere, right alongside the angels and the jewelry. Of course, if you're just looking for a Band-Aid because you have a blister, you're flat out of luck."

That morning I knew that the Grand Canyon, balloon rides, educational opportunities, and time running out notwithstanding, the next summer we'd be back in Vermont.

SIX

PANCAKES, AS I HAVE SAID, WERE PART OF OUR ROUTINE AT the lodge . . . pancakes when we were there, even more than cows while we were on the way. They weren't those little tiny pancakes that you eat by the dozen, but substantial, fat pancakes almost too big for the plate and so full of whatever you wanted in them — almost always chocolate chips in Kip's case, blueberries and, by then, sometimes even walnuts for me — that they nearly fell apart. Pancakes that you'd eat and eat and still there'd be a meal's worth on your plate and you couldn't imagine that you'd have any room for lunch or ever want to look at a pancake again, until the next morning at the breakfast table.

They were, as I think I've also said, best eaten on the porch, on mornings when it was just the kind of still-cool that reminded us of how well we'd slept, wrapped in blankets; mornings when, in the early chill, we cut over through the woods behind the playhouse and ran down the hill to the lodge instead of walking down the dirt road and met Mom and Dad at a table, if we'd already decided where we would eat. There were also mornings when Mom and Kip would start arguing about whether we'd eat on the porch before anybody'd even brushed his or her teeth, and Kip would win. And there were mornings that promised, even if we were the first family on the porch for breakfast, everybody wrapped in a sweater and feeling like a pioneer, that by noon we'd be wishing we could just grab an apple for lunch and run into the lake to cool off.

If you knew the place, you could feel all that just driving to the lodge, and you could feel the springy boards of the old dining room under your feet and hear them creak. You could close your eyes and see the view of the mountains that you'd earn if you hiked up the trail behind the new cabins with your canteen clunking against your leg and trekked across the meadow where there was plenty of evidence that cows had grazed, though there were never any cows. You could hear the slap of the screen door in the playhouse and the "tock-tock-tock" of Ping-Pong games that reminded you to run in and call "Next!" You could remember — or I could by then — the feel of the spines of the old, beat-up books in the room at the end of the lodge that they called the library, where you could hide on a rainy afternoon, or maybe after dinner, and find a copy of the same book you'd left home on the floor, spine up, beside your bed, only it would be an older copy with a cover that was ripped or missing and somebody's long-ago crayoned picture of the yellow sun, green grass, and a brown cow with only two legs on what should have been the blank page at the back. But it would be the same story, and you'd find it and settle into a big, leather chair with it until your little sister came to get you.

I could have remembered all those things as we drove the familiar road toward the lodge the summer after Arizona, listening to our familiar tapes. I could have been thinking about them. But instead I was thinking about the calliope music I'd heard, and the sign that said CIRCUS, the little girl I could now be only almost sure I thought I'd maybe seen, and the way the woods I had been so sure I knew had turned upside down on me that day and dumped me out toward the top of the hill that I was sure I'd been climbing down.

Maybe that was why I fouled up the trip almost from the start. Or at least from before we'd gotten to the lodge. Earlier than ever before, hours before we saw our first cow, I pushed Kip's feet away on the seat and told her to stay on her own side. When the Roald Dahl tape finished and Kip picked *Stuart Little* to play next, I held my ears, rolled my eyes, and said, "Not *Stuart Little*. Please, *any*thing but *Stuart Little*."

"But it's my turn," Kip whined.

"Sure," I said, "but you liked the tape I picked with my turn. You like the Roald Dahl stories better than I do, anyway."

"I thought you liked *Stuart Little*," Kip pouted.

"Stuart Little is Mickey Mouse with better grammar," I said.

From the driver's seat Dad laughed. Kip did, too.

"What are you laughing about?" I snapped. "You don't even know what grammar is. And besides, you like Mickey Mouse *and* Stuart Little."

"Take it easy," Mom said.

"I do not!" Kip shouted. "I hate them both. They're stupid. Let's play the Roald Dahl tape again."

I picked up my book. "Play anything you want," I said. "But get your feet off my side of the car."

"She hit me!" Kip shrieked.

I hadn't. I'd just pushed her feet. She'd have known if I'd hit her. Besides, she was usually the one who hit me. She'd ball up her fist and thunk me in the back. It never hurt much and it always meant that I'd won the fight.

"Well," Dad said, "it'll be great to get to Vermont and have you two spend a week sharing a bedroom. Maybe they'll have a double bed for you. That way it'll be a fight about whose feet are where every night."

It wouldn't be. We'd get along fine, I was sure, even if we had to share a bed, which I knew we wouldn't. It was just the hours in the car, and maybe that my feet were bigger than they'd been and my legs were longer, and Kip was bigger, too. Maybe it was also the woman who read the *Stuart Little* tape. I was sure that if that woman had knocked on our door to sell a magazine subscription or collect money to buy an end-of-school gift for the crossing guard, she'd have used the same words and said them the same way as on the tape, trapped in the stupid story of a mouse who wore a little jacket and boots and fell hopelessly in love with a stupid canary.

But we'd get along fine. We didn't fight in Vermont much, and when we did the fights didn't last. There were too many other things to do. But this time I wasn't thinking about what I'd do with Kip or how I'd help one of the littler kids tie decorations around a walking stick or draw something smaller so it looked further away. I wasn't even thinking about all the things I'd have to tell Snow about the two years now since we'd last seen her, or how she'd smile over how much I'd grown without saying anything stupid about it.

It was the woods I was thinking of, and how quickly I could get into them by myself, and what I'd find when I did.

The silence of no tape seemed to slow down the ride, so in a way I wished I'd never said anything about *Stuart Little*, but it was too late to back down on that one. From my side of the back seat, which I'd defined by piling up three tape boxes, Kip's sneakers, and a carton of Kleenex, I looked out the window. By then we were off the highway, but not yet into the real mountains. I guess I'd never paid much attention to this stretch of the trip before. I must have seen some of the same landscape out the same car window, but when had it ever been so gray? The fight, the quiet, the stupid pile of stuff in the middle of the suddenly small and scratchy back seat, and now the overcast afternoon might have had a lot to do with it, but Vermont didn't look so good. There were junk cars in the yards we passed, and the houses looked junky, too: ranches that needed painting and weren't going to get it. Some of the front porches were wrapped in sheets of dirty plastic against last winter's wind or the wind from the winter before that. On more than one porch there were automobile seats, the porch furniture of last resort, I guessed. There were trailers, too, on blocks, like some of the cars. I saw discarded toys, broken (you could tell, even from a distance and passing quickly) and fallen bikes with bent wheels and, in one case, a faded, pink streamer trailing from the handlebar grip — only one handlebar grip.

This was also the land of hand-lettered signs, but these signs didn't say CIRCUS. They said WELDING or FIRE WOOD or SYRUP or BODY SHOP, or, most optimistically, ANTIQUES.

On previous trips, Kip and I had counted license plates lots of times. It was a great spot for the game. There were always lots of out-of-state license plates in Vermont. But this trip, with Kip silent on her half of the back seat and me defiant on mine, I might have counted the signs. How many people along a single mile of shacks and trailers could make a living pulling and pounding the dents out of old cars? Did they sell the firewood to *one another*? Or did somebody come down from the lodge in a shiny truck once every two weeks, examine the firewood offerings of a dozen hopeful woodsmen, and choose only the best cherry and oak for the blaze that would warm and delight the cross-country skiers in the glowing living room that night?

We'd gone to Vermont only in the summer, but each year the family that owned the lodge sent us a Christmas card that showed the big fireplace hung with stockings. On a table, front and center, was an enormous punch bowl. In front of it were cut-glass mugs. "Season's Greetings" read the message, so as to include everyone. I wondered what the people who lived behind the flapping sheets of plastic thought as they rattled and skidded down the hill past the lodge and toward home, or if they even saw it anymore. I wondered if they'd ever heard the creak of their own boot steps on the wraparound porch or sat, even for a minute, in one of the big rockers painted bright white or forest green. (Maybe they had to come in through the kitchen. Maybe they just dumped the firewood out back in the shed and got paid later.) Coming back to their cars, did they look out over the hill, down to the lake — frozen in winter — and beyond that to the mountains? And did they think it was beautiful? Or when they stood like that in the snow, with the next snow starting to fall, were they just listening for the skidding tires of some city driver's van or Volvo — somebody they could drag out of the ditch for grocery money?

The summer seemed easy, with berries on the bushes and baby-sitting money for the teenagers. On rainy days tourists like us nosed around the barns and shops, buying old kitchen chairs, rusty farm tools, handmade sweaters, and maple sugar candy. But in the winter, how many of the skiers racing between mountains bothered to stop for arts and crafts?

When Kip and I were littler, on days when I complained that there was nothing to do and Kip fell in line and said so too, Mom would sometimes tell us how, when she was a little girl, she would watch people go by on the street and make up stories about them: this man who'd just turned around was hurrying because he'd suddenly remembered that he'd forgotten to set the parking brake on his car and he was afraid that if he didn't get back and do it his new DeSoto would buck once and then roll down the hill where he lived. And the woman shouting at the little boy in the red cap? She wasn't really his mother. She'd married the boy's father for his money and was only enduring the child's company until he was old enough to send away to school. Meanwhile, the older man looking in the window of the jewelry store was thinking about how surprised and delighted his lady friend in New York would be if he were to show up that weekend with a shining diamond engagement ring. She'd throw her arms around his neck. She'd call her mother in Nebraska and tell her through tears that her dreams had come true.

I could have made up stories like that about the children in the yards of the cabins and shacks we passed on the sides of the hills, or about the deaf uncles and dozing grandmothers I couldn't see inside. Kip would have joined in. But on that day I didn't. After we'd passed by, taking our stories with us, the children, uncles, grandmothers, widows, and self-employed body shop men would still have been right where they'd been that morning, when they'd woken up coughing or sure they'd dreamed the winning lottery numbers, if they could get in to the 7-Eleven to buy a ticket.

Normally, either Kip or I or both of us would get tired of the silence. After we fought, she'd ask me what I was reading and wonder if I'd read it out loud. Or one of us would have to go to the bathroom and we'd both start looking for a gas station and working together to convince Mom and Dad that we should get potato chips, a chocolate bar, or at least sodas when we found the place to stop.

One of them would say, "*Then* we'll have to stop so you can go to the bathroom *again*."

One of us would say, "But I'm really thirsty."

One of them would say, "All right. You can split a soda."

One of us would point out that we didn't like the same kind.

One of them would do what they both called a "Ralph Cramden," winding up with a fist and saying either "One of these days, Alice" or "You want to go to the moon?" (I had no idea what that was all about until years later, when I saw some of the old black and white Jackie Gleason *Honeymooners* episodes, but I knew even at the time that it was just a joke. Nobody was going to clobber anybody else. Nobody was going to the moon. I also knew that we'd get the soda — root beer and orange, probably, and the potato chips and chocolate bar, too. We just had to go through the ritual first.)

On this trip, though, we must have brought enough snacks and kept the juice packs to a minimum. In the silence of no tape, we just drove, Kip eventually falling asleep on her side of the back seat and me alone on mine, first surprised when the sunlight found a different angle through my window and showed me how much of the curly hair on the back on my dad's head had gone gray, and then a little sad at that.

On that trip we arrived at the lodge late in the afternoon. Snow would have been gone for hours. She was only at the playhouse in the mornings. While we were eating lunch on our cabin porches or at the lodge, she'd be putting away everything we'd promised we wouldn't leave out. If we wandered back past the playhouse on the way to the lake in the afternoon, we'd find it locked. Kip knew that as well as I did, but as soon as we stopped the car in front of the lodge to check in, she jumped out, slammed the back door, and shouted, "I'm going to see if Snow's here!"

On that trip we had one of the newer cabins, so we were back in the woods, not on the hill overlooking the lodge. The floor of that cabin didn't tip and the porch didn't creak. Since there'd have been no sense in building a new cabin with a bathtub that stood alone and had claws at the end of its stumpy legs, this cabin had a shower. It had carpeting instead of rag rugs, too. It was bright and open rather than comfy, and instead of standing in a row of identical cabins, it was off in the woods by itself.

When she'd caught up with us at the cabin after finding the playhouse locked, racing through the parking lot to see if Snow's truck was there, and then asking at the desk to make sure that, yes, of course she still worked at the lodge and would be back the next morning, Kip said she hated the new place.

"It's not like a cabin at all," she complained. "It's just a house. We could have stayed home."

We were in the bedroom we'd share for the week. "What's

the difference?" I said. "All we'll do is sleep here and eat sandwiches on the porch. And you got as tired of baths as I did when we were up on the hill. This place has a shower."

"It's not a cabin, though," Kip said. She ran her hand along the smooth wallboard, painted light blue. "Look. I don't even think it's made of wood."

"Good," I said. "That means the spiders won't like it as well." But the truth was that I was a little disappointed, too. I wondered what else would be different this time.

SEVEN

THAT NIGHT, AFTER EVERYBODY'D GONE TO SLEEP, I
found out.

I woke up to the sound of calliope music. It wasn't loud,
but it was unmistakable. At first, before I was entirely awake,
I thought Mom and Dad had left a radio on. But of course
even in the new cabins there were no radios. That and no
TV was part of the point of going to Vermont. Mom and
Dad said it all the time.

I turned over in my bed and looked at Kip. In the moonlight coming through the window, I could see that she'd
kicked her sheet into a ball at the end of her bed and turned
herself around so that she was sideways on the mattress. One
leg was draped over the side of the bed. She might wake up
on the floor, which would give her a story to tell at breakfast.

I sat up in my bed and rubbed my eyes. Outside, from the
direction of the lake, a loon called. *Another creature that's up
too early,* I remember thinking. I padded to the window

between our beds and leaned against the screen. The moon, almost full, was bright against a band of clouds. Our window faced the woods, and there wasn't much space between the back of the cabin and the trees: maybe a few yards. That space was filled with fireflies. I'd read somewhere or been told that their blinking lights were part of a courtship dance. They lit up their bottoms to attract mates. We never saw them at home. Mom said that was probably because of the chemicals everybody put on their lawns to make sure the grass stayed green no matter what.

If it *was* a mating dance I was seeing, Vermont — or at least the lodge — would have a record number of fireflies next time around. The little winking lights were everywhere. They bobbed and darted in the stillness of the night. I stepped into my sandals and crept out to get a better look. I opened the screen door that led to the deck just far enough so that I could see through it sideways. I wanted the moonlight and the fireflies to myself. I would have said that was why I was stepping out into the night.

Another loon cried, lonely and spooky. I wondered if they were mating, too. If so, they didn't sound too thrilled about it, as if they thought that only more sadness was bound to come from babies.

In the yard behind the cabin, I could have caught fireflies in my hand if I'd wanted to do it. The calliope music from the woods was louder there, but still so soft that I had to stop walking through the grass to be sure I heard it. I hadn't re-membered seeing a path out back that evening when we'd arrived, but now, in the moonlight, there seemed to be one, or at least the beginning of one. I thought I'd go in just a little ways.

It's easy to say that I should have stayed in bed, or that if I'd insisted on going outside, I should have been content to listen to the music from a distance, the way I listened to the loon. I even thought, as I stood at the edge of the woods, that someday when I had a daughter of my own I'd tell her not to go following the calliope music into the woods all by herself when she should be sleeping safely in a room right next to mine.

Of course, I pictured that little girl whom I'd one day wisely advise as much younger than I was then. I looked back once at the cabin, neat and safe in the clearing, full of the people I loved, and I started down the path.

Horns joined the calliope then, and a high-pitched, whistling instrument, too, like a flute. Almost at once, they all sounded much nearer, and I didn't even have to look back to know that if I had I wouldn't have seen the cabin but only the woods closed behind me.

If you walk in woods where there is no hunting and never has been, sometimes you can step into a clearing and surprise a deer. (Not a tractor, like the one in Arizona, but a real deer, light brown and white, with big eyes.) Kip and I did it once on Cuttyhunk, an island near Martha's Vineyard. If you're lucky, you and the deer will just stand there looking at each other, wondering, maybe, which one is more amazed.

That's just the way it was with the dancer in the pink dress and me.

I didn't recognize her right away. She had her back to me, and she was standing on one leg — her left. She'd raised her right leg straight over her head, and, with one hand on the thigh of the raised leg and the other way up on the ankle, she seemed to be trying to point the way to the moon. Her neck was bent forward and her hair, wonderfully black against the pink of her dress, hung across her face. She couldn't have noticed me, I thought, or she wouldn't have stayed in that defenseless position. Even a deer that wasn't going to run would have prepared herself to do it.

But I was wrong. While she was still on the toes of one foot, still stretching toward the stars, she spoke.

"Hello," she said. "You've come back."

"You remember me?"

Slowly she brought her leg down. She'd turned as she was doing it, and now she faced me, one hand on her hip. Though she had looked impossibly long and narrow in her pose, she was no taller than I, or not much. She was dark-eyed and sure of herself this time.

"You are memorable," she said. "Come along."

"Where are we going?" I asked her. I'd come into the woods on my own because it was where I wanted to go, but who knew what that meant?

She turned, and I followed her in the starlight. Wherever we were going, she knew the way, even at night. Maybe only at night. We seemed to be walking toward the music, which was as happy as ever.

"Are you like a sentry?" I asked.

"I'm a dancer," she said, still walking. Then, over her shoulder, without slowing down, she asked me or the sky, "I wonder if you'll be a dancer, too?"

"I think I want to be a teacher," I said. "Maybe first grade or kindergarten."

I thought I heard her giggle at that, but I wasn't sure. By then the music was loud enough to fill the woods — a whole circus band of music — and I realized that under the calliope, the horns, and the whistling flute, I'd been hearing a bass drum for some time. They played the traditional, welcome-to-the-circus music: Dit-dit-diddle-diddle-dit-dit-da-da, dit-dit-diddle-diddle-dit-dit-da-da, boom, di-da-da, boom, di-da-da, dit-dit-diddle-diddle-dah-dah-dah-dah. At any moment I expected to hear somebody shout in a deep voice "Step right up!" but nobody did.

When I was so young that Kip hadn't been born yet, maybe three, Mom and Dad took me to my first circus. It was not a full-fledged big top, just a junior sort of circus, but it was under a tent just the same, maybe the first tent I'd ever been under. I don't know whether I remember that day or only think I do because they reminded me about it so often. They told the story with a sweetness and sadness that I didn't understand for a long time, and for a moment each time I heard it, I would miss being a little girl and feel glad that I was one no longer, both at once.

"It was a hot afternoon," Dad said, "and stuffy in the tent. It smelled like the animals. Just after we found our seats, the lights went out. In the quiet before the band started to play, I heard this little voice beside me. 'How long do we have to stay?' That was what you asked us."

"I didn't like the circus?"

"I think you didn't like the dark," Dad said. "And it was hot. Summer in a tent."

"You didn't like loud noises," Mom said. "Sometimes when you were little, we'd walk around the neighborhood to see what all the noises were before you could relax. We'd have to go see the truck that was unloading gravel where they were building a new house, or the backyard where some older children were shooting baskets and shouting."

"Even the refrigerator," Dad said, laughing. "If we were putting you to bed and it kicked on, you'd put your finger to your lips and say, 'Shush, fridger.' I think in that tent you must have known the band was going to crash into action at any moment, and that was a little spooky."

"So I didn't like the circus?"

"You didn't like that one much," Mom said. "We didn't stay long. When you were older, remember you and Dad and Kip went to the big circus — Barnum and Bailey? You loved that. You came home with a big program full of pictures of acrobats, bareback riders, and clowns. We all looked at it together for weeks."

"What about Kip?" I asked. "Did she hate noises?"

"Kip was born into noise and confusion," Mom said.

"Certainly," Dad agreed. "*You* were already here."

• • •

This circus was different, and not just because I'd wandered out to find it by myself. Not just because there was a dancer my own size showing me the way, either, while my parents slept in our cabin and Kip dreamt of chocolate chip pancakes. As far as I could tell, this circus seemed to twist in the dark through the woods. There was no mistaking it for the big top. There was nowhere to pay to get in. The little dancer and I were one minute among the trees and then suddenly alongside a long, canvas wall covered in faded paintings of mysteries and freaks. There was a cartoony drawing of a cow with two heads, and a big picture in which a boy with no legs and flippers instead of arms smiled as if life were just grand. A little further along the canvas, it said SEE NATURE'S MISTAKES in huge red letters, also faded, and there were more pictures: one showed a man reading a book, dressed in a summer-weight suit, with a long, bushy tail coming out of the back of his pants, while a dog with little horns on its head gazed stupidly up at him.

"Will we see these?" I asked the dancer.

"Not tonight," she said. "Another time, maybe. Goodness knows they're not going anywhere. Right now I have to rehearse. It's good you arrived when you did. You can watch."

That was a funny thing to hear, since I'd thought she'd been waiting in the woods for me.

"The other time I saw you," I said. "Why did you run away from me?"

Her big, dark eyes got wider. "Did I?" she asked. "Or did you run away from me?"

"I was lost in the woods," I said.

"But now you're found," she said. "You'll see." She took my hand then, and before long we were in front of a tent at least as big as the one that had been too dark and hot for me in the story Mom and Dad told. "If anybody gives you a hard time, just tell them you're with me. I'm Antoinette. Everybody calls me Toni."

"I'm Molly," I told her.

"And happy to be so, I'm sure," she said. "After a fashion."

With that she pulled aside the tent flap I hadn't seen before, and together we went in. There wasn't much chance that anyone inside would give me any trouble. There wasn't much chance that anyone would even notice me. Dozens of performers, lots of them no older than Toni, ran this way and that over the sawdust-covered ground. From the edges of the tent to the very top stretched hundreds of strings of colored lights. Their reflections shimmered off the costumes of the performers and made even the few who were standing still seem to flow and glide.

Toni ran to a rope ladder that hung from a tiny platform impossibly high overhead. (Inside, the tent seemed much larger than it had appeared to be as we'd come up on it — in fact, from the inside it looked larger than any clearing in those woods could have held.) I watched as she climbed effortlessly, though the rope ladder bounced and swung above and below her. Up she went, and I was astonished to see that

the air into which she was climbing was already full of acrobats. They outnumbered the people on the ground by a score
or more. Even under the biggest big top, there shouldn't
have been room for them all, and yet they swung and sailed
across the tent, leaving one trapeze for another just when it
seemed as if they'd waited too long and would have to swing
back to where they'd started and try again. They sailed
across the crowded space and, thank goodness, nobody ever
seemed to miss. They turned somersaults in the air, found
with their ankles somebody's fingertips at the end of every
airborne tumble, and came up each time smiling to the
crowd that wasn't there, except for me.

There were no nets.

Within just a few minutes I'd lost Toni in the sky of the
tent. She must have been up there among the most coura-
geous performers, so far above the floor of the tent that,
looking up, I couldn't tell her pink costume from somebody
else's red or lavender. A couple of times in the swing and
flash of lithe bodies through the air I thought I'd found her
again, but then each time I wasn't sure. When looking up for
so long had made me dizzy, I sat back in the empty bleacher.

When we'd entered the tent, I'd only noticed the acrobats,
like Toni. Running and jumping, climbing and then flying,
they seemed to need and fill all the space in the tent. But now
I noticed that they — we — weren't alone. Opposite the
bleacher where I sat, a dozen young men, all in bright body
suits, were rehearsing *their* act, an ever-changing, always

more ambitious human pyramid. The men at the top of the pile were constantly scuttling down over the shoulders and thighs of the men at the bottom, who were continuously clambering up over the hips and straining necks of the men on the way down. I couldn't believe they could do it, even as I saw it happening. The pyramid itself, when you weren't looking right at it, seemed motionless, solid and firm.

I left my place in the bleacher and walked toward them. The closer I got, the more impossible the spectacle seemed to be. The men scuttling up the pyramid should have been hitting the men over whom they were climbing in the eyes, noses, and chins with their hard knees, elbows, and heads. Men on the way down the pyramid should have been landing on the floor of the tent with thuds and grunts. Instead, all the movement seemed choreographed, impossibly smooth.

I was fascinated. Each man was a crucial part in the constant motion of the machine, which was growing at exactly the same rate that it was shrinking. Every performer helped hold up every other. Without any one of them, the pyramid would have been just a pile. Or at least I thought I'd figured out that much about the exercise, until one of the men involved in the mysterious making and unmaking of the pyramid suddenly leapt out of the process, turned a perfect backflip, and landed just a few feet from where I stood.

I called them men, but this one, like Toni, was younger. He wasn't much older than I, but he had a man's shoulders, and his legs were thick and strong. His hair was longish and brown, his eyes deep blue. He should have been panting, but he wasn't. He stood before me casually. We might have been meeting at a bus stop.

"I hope you're enjoying the show," he said, "even though this isn't the show proper, of course. They call me Jimmy the Monkey. Who are you?"

Before I could tell him, there came these warning words from the sky: "She's only visiting, Jimmy."

We both looked up. Toni had swung down out of the continuous sweep and tumble of the acrobats. Hanging by her heels from a shining silver bar, she'd passed just over our heads to deliver her message and had come so close that she hadn't had to speak much above a whisper. All the other acrobats were far above Toni, and even as we watched she was sailing up again toward a tiny and distant platform mounted on a sky-high pole. She might have waved as she went.

"Oh," said Jimmy the Monkey. "Sorry."

"For what?" I asked. I needn't have bothered. Before the words had left my mouth, he'd leapt back into his ever-changing slot in the pyramid. Even as I looked, I lost him. Right there on the ground, he was as hard to follow as Toni was overhead.

If Toni was protecting me from something, she hadn't said what it was. She hadn't told me to stay where I was and wait for her to come down, either, so I decided to look around a bit more on my own. Jimmy the Monkey certainly hadn't minded my watching. Maybe nobody else would. It *was* a circus.

No surprise, then, that there were tigers now at the center of the tent, though I hadn't noticed them before. If you've been to the circus, you've seen the lions and tigers. A man wearing a tarzan-type suit and cracking a whip sets them to doing tricks. They climb up on colored boxes or follow one another around at his commands. Tigers move magnificently, whatever they're moving to do, but when the lion and tiger tamer barks at them and cocks his hand, they shrink from him and from themselves, too, as if they are a little ashamed.

At the center of *this* ring, the tigers glared. As much as it was possible to do under a circus tent, they prowled. Unlike the tigers in the zoo, which usually seem to me to have given up, these tigers didn't appear to require any more space than they had. Their coats were full and bright, their eyes an astonishing green. Toni was light on her feet and quick in the air. Jimmy the Monkey was square as a block across the shoulders and his legs were knots of hard muscle. But these tigers . . . these tigers were power and grace.

Up close (I was close to them now, close enough to see their whiskers twitch and follow their eyes as they followed mine), they were also big. I found myself wondering if a tiger could knock me down with a flick of his apparently lazy tail.

There were three of them, and they seemed much less interested in me than I was in them. They stretched, and one of them turned magnificently and yawned. I was closest to him, and his tongue was pale pink. His teeth didn't sparkle; this was not a cartoon. But the tiger licked them. Had it occurred to him to eat me up? Now I was close enough to hear him exhale and feel that his breath was warm and moist.

I wasn't afraid of him. He was astonishing, and to fear him seemed absurd. He was wonderful.

There was no trainer anywhere.

"Of course," I said to the tiger nearest me, the one who'd yawned, "you don't have to jump up on a box or leap through a hoop. You don't have to raise your paw as if you were begging or shake your head and growl upon command. You don't have to do anything but be a tiger."

The tiger walked toward me, rippling. I was used to cute animals: kittens with names like Mandy and Muffin and golden retriever puppies for sale, climbing over each other and tumbling out of their box. This tiger was long and muscled. He moved with what I later came to understand as the grace of the disdainful. He didn't care if I liked him or not, and he was no more afraid of me than I was of him. He passed by me, close enough to brush my leg, but he didn't shift to touch me. I turned and watched him for a moment as his shoulders rolled and he padded away from me, across the floor of the tent. He seemed to be heading for an opening in the canvas, which I hadn't noticed earlier. I followed him.

Outside it would still have been dark, except that along that portion of the tent ran a line of bright, flaming torches. The tiger turned left along the row. He walked past a troop of child jugglers, or that's what I thought at first. As one of the torches flared, I noticed that they were dwarves. Their features were coarse in the firelight, but their hands were quick and their concentration on the flying balls and duck-pins that they tossed to one another and caught and returned or spun off confidently to somebody else was marvelous. One of them — the one wearing a gray fedora and red fire-man's suspenders to hold up his suit pants — grunted softly as he made his tosses, as if it were more work for him. The rest of them went quietly about what they were doing. Nobody shouted "Tiger on the loose!" Nobody said anything. One of them — the one who was bald and barefoot and had long, curly hair on his gnarled, fat toes — glanced at me as I watched, unless it was only a trick of the flickering light. If he did look, it wasn't for long, or he'd have been cracked in the head or the elbow by one of the flying objects. Watching them, I couldn't imagine any of them missing. Not even the one who grunted a little.

I'd paused there only briefly, but I'd paused for too long. When I looked away from the jugglers, the tiger was gone. He hadn't been impressed at all.

I hurried along in the direction he'd been walking, hoping I'd catch sight of the end of his twitching tail. I realized that I'd assumed he'd been leading me somewhere, though there was no reason I should have thought this.

At the corner of the tent, which I reached before I thought I would, the last torch in the long line blazed. Ahead of me in the darkness there was no tiger. I looked back. There were no dwarves. But beyond the edge of the woods, which ran up almost to the tent at this place in the clearing, I thought I could see another flickering light.

Toni had met me when I'd walked into the woods much earlier that night. She'd even seemed to expect me. Jimmy the Monkey had stepped free of the living pyramid, which didn't look as if it could do without him. He'd introduced himself, and he'd certainly looked as if he'd have kept me company, given half a chance. But Toni had swooped down and batted that chance away. The tiger had felt like a test: Would I have the courage to stand and admire him, even as he walked by close enough for me to pet him? I'd passed, if that was the point, though out of wonder rather than bravery. But maybe it wasn't a test at all. Who would have been testing me?

I'd followed the tiger as the tiger had seemed to intend, but maybe he hadn't at all. I couldn't remember him looking back at me. Maybe he didn't know I was following him, or didn't care. Toni hadn't interfered when I'd left the tent, which made me feel then as if that had been an acceptable decision. Wouldn't she have stepped between me and danger?

But maybe not. Maybe she was just jealous of the attention I'd drawn from Jimmy the Monkey, whose grin I could still see, but not of the tiger, nonchalant and contemptuous. Or maybe she'd been flying through the air with the greatest of ease in the other direction. Or maybe she just hadn't been paying attention. Why should she have been looking out for me, anyway? It hadn't been her idea for me to wander off into the woods, had it?

I suppose I could have followed my own tracks back the way I'd come, along the line of the tent. The jugglers were gone, unless they were around a corner I hadn't noticed I was turning, but why shouldn't the opening through which I'd left the tent be there if I retraced my steps? And if I found myself back inside, wouldn't Jimmy the Monkey, whose curly, brown hair I could recall quite well, too, still be exchanging places with the boys above and below him? Wouldn't Toni still be sailing overhead, or maybe even looking for me, and just a little anxiously by now?

I took a deep breath of the clear night air. Maybe Toni had forgotten me. Maybe Jimmy the Monkey was only thinking about ice cream or cotton candy as he scrambled up and down. Maybe the tiger with his green eyes shining would have walked away from the ring and out of the tent and off into whatever invisible distance he'd found whether I'd been there or not. Maybe there had been no plan at all.

I started toward the light I could see flickering through the trees.

Some of the woods around the lodge looked wild, and they weren't without dangers. In the wrong season you could get poison ivy if you weren't paying attention, and roots as thick as a fire hose crisscrossed some of the paths. In a hurry to get to the lake, you could trip over them and tumble or roll until you came up against a tree or skidded to a stop in the dirt. Kip and I had been skinned and stunned often enough that Mom said once we should wear our Rollerblading helmets and elbow pads when we hiked down to the lake. But the paths were easy to learn, Snow was an excellent teacher, and any trail meant to take you somewhere was marked and tended.

Not in the woods surrounding the circus tent. The flickering light was there, except when it didn't seem to be, but while I could have confidently walked the paths near the lodge and the lake even in the dark, here there was only a hint of a trail where somebody might have walked before. At one step I could feel my foot crash through a tangle of vines, and, pulling it out, I'd find myself lurching off sideways in a direction that the path, such as it was, hadn't suggested at all. Then I'd get a few easy steps in, only to lose sight of the distant fire, and then almost bang up against a tree or a bush as thick as a hedge.

The moon helped a little. I didn't actually crash into anything. The firelight gave me something to aim for. But otherwise I was on my own in a way I'd never been before. I've thought about that part of the night lots of times since. Always it seems to me that I should have been frightened. Was it that nothing could frighten me then? That my parents had lent me confidence over the years, showing me what was making all the noises? Was it the feeling of the lodge itself, safe as the cozy back seat of the car felt at the familiar beginning of each trip north? Was it what Snow had taught us about where the paths led? Maybe it didn't matter. Off I'd gone.

For a while I didn't seem to be getting any closer to the fire, although I'd certainly gotten farther away from the tent. When I turned, I couldn't see it. The calliope music still beeped and hooted in the woods, though more softly than before. I remember thinking, as I checked back over my shoulder from time to time, that even hearing the music, somebody coming from this direction would have a hard time finding the circus. The woods were that dark and thick.

The ground here was flat, but the tree roots beat at my toes and the knee-high shrubs and bushes pulled at my legs. I'd read about shipwrecked sailors trying to swim against the tide toward shore, kicking with their legs and pulling with their arms, becoming more and more exhausted with each worthless stroke, and, as far as they could tell, getting no closer to land at all. It was the kind of thought that could have frightened me into running, which would have been about the dumbest thing I could have done. I'd have tripped, sprawled, and cracked my head open on a rock or fallen down a ravine nobody even knew was there. At least I might have. And the juggling dwarves might have been five hundred yards behind me, but they might have been a mile back, too. In either case, they'd paid no attention to me when I'd seen them at the corner of the tent, and they were at least as unprepared as I was for crashing through the underbrush.

"But now you're found," Toni had said. I'd never felt less found or more lost.

Then, with a suddenness that I could no more explain than a sleeper, waking, could tell you the time, I was before the fire that I'd been moving toward and losing and, apparently, heading for again. It was a tame fire, much smaller than it had seemed to be from a distance. Over it, from an iron rod supported by two forked sticks, hung a pot. Not a caldron or anything, just a dented, metal pot. Somebody was here, or had been. And even as I watched, she came back.

EIGHT

THE FIRST THING I NOTICED ABOUT HER WAS THE WAY HER red hair, which curled halfway down her back, gleamed in the firelight as she approached it. She should have been wearing a black dress, ankle-length. The red of her hair would have been magical against the black. Or a lace blouse — the work of small hands with all the time in the world and traditional patterns to impart — would have been reasonable to expect. But she wore Bermuda shorts — an old pair, full of greens and reds, and the shorts tightened across her broad backside as she leaned over the pot to sniff at it. On her feet she wore flip-flops, which, like the shorts, would have been better for the beach than the woods. After peering into the pot for a moment, she stood up straight, then leaned backward a little on her heels and ran her palms down the small of her back, as if it had hurt her to straighten up.

She grunted —"Ugh, oh. Age and pain"— as she stepped back from the fire and turned around. That was when I could read the lettering on her T-shirt: I ♥ NY. That was when she first saw me, and she jumped.

"Lord, child!" she yelped. And then, "Didn't anybody ever teach you not to sneak up on somebody out of the woods like that? Especially somebody who's old?"

"I'm sorry," I said.

"You probably thought I already knew you were there," she said. "Probably thought you couldn't startle a fortune-teller, since she'd already know you were coming."

I hadn't thought about that, but now I did. What she said made sense, at least as much as fortunetelling made sense. Maybe she wasn't a very good fortuneteller.

"I'm as good as most and better than some," she said with a smile. "Got you that time, eh?"

I was still standing at the edge of the little clearing where the fire burned. Now she beckoned me forward. Her face was tanned and healthy-looking. Not so old as all that. Around her neck she wore a silver chain. You might have expected there to be a yin-yang charm or an amulet of some kind on it, but it was just silver links.

"Just the chain," she said, and she winked. "Ha! Got you again."

And she had.

"What are you after?" she asked.

"Don't tell me you know I'm wondering why you asked me that," I said, the words coming out very quickly.

"I'm sorry," she said. "I was just having a little fun with you. No harm meant."

"No harm done," I said. "And the answer to your question, in case you really don't already have it, is that I don't know."

She was moving away from the fire as we talked, and I was moving with her. I hadn't noticed her wagon before — a wooden trailer at the other end of the clearing. It was red, but it hadn't been painted for a long time. She indicated its steps as a place to sit, and together we settled there.

"Tell me more," she said. She leaned back on her elbows, so that the small of her back rested against the next-to-top step, just below the door to the wagon's cabin, through which she seemed in no special hurry to go.

"I saw the sign that said CIRCUS. That's where it started," I said.

The fortuneteller nodded. "When was that? And how much more have you seen?"

"Not this summer or the last, but the one before that. And the sign was the only thing that time, except for a glimpse of Toni."

"Antoinette," she said. "Yes."

"You know her?"

She nodded. "It's not such a large circus," she said. "Though it may seem so to you now."

"Big enough to turn me around a few times," I said.

"So Antoinette found you again today? And this is only the second time?"

"I thought I'd found her," I said.

The fortuneteller shrugged. "Who else?"

"Jimmy the Monkey," I said. "And I followed a tiger out of the tent and saw some dwarves juggling, but none of them paid any attention to me and I don't know their names."

"And now me," she said. "I'm Nell."

"I'm Molly," I told her, and I stuck out my hand, intending to take hers firmly, as I'd been taught to do. Nell looked surprised for a moment, then she took my hand. Her grip was firm, too.

"I'm pleased to meet you, Molly," she said. Then she frowned. "Don't put much stock in that Jimmy the Monkey. Any of them might be named that. Perhaps all of them are. There's not a dime's worth of difference between 'em, whatever they call themselves."

At that she nonchalantly produced a new dime from her right hand. She gently laid the coin in my palm, which was still outstretched.

"Nell of the shiny dimes," she said. "It'll be easier for you to remember."

But I would have remembered. Her wagon there in the clearing was the first place I'd had a chance to catch my breath since Toni had led me to the tent. In the quiet moment on Nell's steps, the acrobats and Toni herself, the pyramid climbers, the tiger, the dwarves — they all seemed as unlikely as they would have from the familiar peace and quiet of my bed in the room I was sharing with Kip before I'd decided to walk into the woods earlier that night — how many hours before?

"What time is it?" I asked Nell.

"Here or there?"

"What do you mean?"

She stretched her legs on the steps. "There you have hours," she said. "Are they all the same length?"

"Yes," I said, without hesitation.

"So an hour in the dentist's chair is the same as an hour at a birthday party? A really good birthday party, now, with all your best friends there and nobody ganging up on anybody else, and the cake homemade and filling the whole house with its wonderful smell?"

"I see what you mean," I said.

"I don't think you do," said Nell. "You think I mean the hour at the party seems shorter than the hour with the dentist at work on your tooth. I'm asking you to think about whether it *is* shorter. And what about the hours when you're asleep? How fast do they go by?"

"They seem to go by very quickly."

"Seem to? Or do?" She pointed to the moon, then, and smiled back at me. "How long has the moon been right there in that night sky?"

"Right there? The moon isn't 'right there' ever, is it? The moon's going around the earth. The earth's circling the sun. Nothing in the sky or anywhere else is ever 'right there' for any time at all."

"Science," Nell sniffed. "I once knew an old woman who didn't know as much about the movement of the spheres as you've explained in two sentences, but she could turn a dog to stone by raising her eyebrow. And that dog, sure as dark, wasn't going anywhere other than 'right there' for a long, long time. Who do you think knew more?"

I looked up at the moon. For a while Nell and I just sat. Then all of a sudden she was up on her feet, more agile than I would have thought she could be.

"Now you can come into the wagon," she said. "Unless you don't believe in that, either."

"Believe in what?" I asked.

"Fortunetelling," she said. "Why else would anybody visit an old red-haired woman who lived in the middle of the woods? Especially in the middle of the night? Assuming, of course, that it is the middle of the night. Unless you needed a Band-Aid. I probably have some Band-Aids in there, too."

With that, she opened up the door at the top of the steps, crouched briefly, grunted, and disappeared inside.

Of course I followed her.

Most of the lantern-lit room was taken up by a wooden table covered with a black lace cloth. Nell made her way sideways around the table to an armchair and sat down with another grunt. On the shelves behind her were books, bottles, and brightly painted masks of creatures I didn't recognize, animals with intelligent eyes. Some of them had little ears that might have been horns, but most of them appeared kind, and some were cute. A few had quivering whiskers, like cats. We might have made them in Snow's playhouse, though we'd have needed materials beyond balloons, papier-mâché, and paint.

There were boxes on the shelves, too, of various shapes and sizes, most of them covered with dust. There was no light beside the lantern, though the stubs of two thick white candles sat on the table before Nell.

I sat down in the only other chair, which was straight and hard, and stood opposite Nell's armchair. I looked across the table at Nell, and she looked back at me.

"No crystal ball?" I asked.

Nell opened her eyes wide and began to make swirling motions with her large hands. Then she stopped. "You'd rather have a crystal ball? I can do a crystal ball. I thought maybe you'd find it corny."

"Once I went to a medieval fair with the whole family," I told her, though I hadn't thought about that fair in a long time. "There was an old man with a bushy white beard — real, his own — and he was dressed in the royal robes of a king. There was a queen, too, and jesters, knights, all kinds of characters. They had jousting, and there was middle ages stuff to buy: flowers woven into garlands; swords, of course, and shields; the long, pointy hats with veils hanging down like the ladies trapped in towers wore — at least the ones we saw in books.

"Anyway, there was a gypsy fortuneteller there, or a lady pretending to be a fortuneteller the same way the man in the beard was pretending to be a king. I wandered over to her tent — she had a tent, not a wagon like this — but when I asked her how much to tell my fortune, she wouldn't do it."

Nell cocked her head to one side. "Wouldn't do it?" she

asked. "What do you mean? She had to do it. Or pretend to. She was charging money, wasn't she?"

"Two dollars," I said. "I think you had to pay in tickets, which you bought when you came in. You were stuck with them when you left if you didn't use them up. We used to give them to kids who were staying longer, or coming in when we were leaving."

"Tickets, pieces of eight, coin of the realm," said Nell with one of her shrugs. "She was there to tell fortunes. Paid to do it. Why wouldn't she tell yours?"

"She said I was too young. She told me to come back in another summer."

"Did she take your hand?" Nell asked. She seemed more interested in this story than in anything else I'd had to say.

"She only looked at me," I said. "And she looked at Kip."

"Your sister," Nell said, though I hadn't told her. "Maybe the fortuneteller meant you should come back by yourself, but she didn't want to say it. Didn't want to hurt Kip's feelings."

"She didn't look as if she cared about that," I said.

"Looks!" Nell sniffed. "What can you tell from that? Look at me and you'd think I was a bag lady." She shifted in her chair, leaned forward, put her elbow on the table, and rested her chin on the heel of her hand. "Still, it's curious that she'd pass up the two dollars. Maybe she thought you and Kip were trying to get two fortunes for the price of one."

I didn't know the real reason, either. It had been a funny day. We'd run into traffic on the way to the fair, which had been farther away than my dad had thought. We'd had to park on the far side of a rutted field, which we'd bounced across unhappily — or at least my dad was unhappy with the bouncing, and Kip kept saying she was going to throw up. Maybe the fortuneteller could tell just by looking at me that it would be a bad day for my fortune.

Or maybe Mom or Dad was somewhere in the crowd, watching. Maybe the fortuneteller didn't like that. Kip had been complaining that they wouldn't let us go off on our own at the fair, and they'd finally said, "Oh, all right. Go!" But maybe they were watching. Maybe the fortuneteller didn't want them to know I was having my fortune told. Or maybe she didn't want them to find out whatever it was she would have told me.

"No matter," said Nell. She'd been looking at me across the table. "If I can't figure out what that fairgrounds fake was up to, you certainly can't."

"Does anybody ever get mad when you intercept their thoughts?" I asked.

"Nope." Nell shrugged again. "I've always felt that most people were flattered I'd think their thoughts were interesting enough to intercept." She looked into my eyes again. "You still want a crystal ball?"

"I guess it would be redundant," I said. It was a word I'd just learned, and I was proud to have used it.

"Or at the very least superfluous," Nell said. "Now, is there anything particular you want to know, or shall I just look around in there and tell you what I find?"

" 'Look around in there?' Do you want to take my hand?"

"If you like," said Nell, and she took my right hand in both of hers. Her fingers felt strong. Her eyes never left mine. "You've had it pretty good," she said. And then, almost immediately, "Did you know you once fell over backwards off the edge of a blue sofa and raised a knot on your head the size of an egg?"

"That's in there?"

"Nothing's ever lost," she said. "You scared your parents something fierce that day. You wouldn't stop crying, though it was mostly surprise rather than pain. You didn't know you could fall when they were right there beside you. Babies hate learning that."

"Maybe they should have been paying more attention," I said. I felt like I was watching a movie.

"They thought so, too," Nell said. "That's why they were so frightened."

"When I was little, I couldn't imagine that anything could frighten Mom and Dad."

Nell let go of my hand. "You're not past learning yet," she said.

"Mom sometimes says I act like I know everything," I said.

Nell nodded. "You can learn from that, too. The scary fact is, you do know a lot. You're a watcher and a listener."

She wasn't telling me anything I hadn't heard, but there was gravity to her words. I knew they were real and true, and no smart aleck remark came to me.

"No," she said. "But I can show you something you haven't seen."

I closed my eyes then because I knew she wanted me to, even though she hadn't said anything. I saw the woods. Not the unfamiliar woods around the tent or the trees at the edge of the clearing where Nell's wagon stood, but the woods I'd walked through with Kip and Mom and Dad, one of us carrying towels, the others with beach chairs and lunch. The woods I had learned from Snow. I was on the path that led from the lodge to the lake.

It was hot at midday, so hot that everybody talked about how it must be *really* hot at home, and how lying on the part of the beach shaded by the trees was the only sensible way to spend the afternoon. There you could lie in such a way that the little lake waves would swirl all the way up past your knees. You could keep your hair dry, if that was what you wanted to do.

It wasn't just hot, though; it was the dry, crackling kind of hot that summer in the north woods can be when it hasn't rained in a long time. It never rained when we were at the lodge, but this summer it hadn't rained before we arrived, either. Or it hadn't rained enough.

"The rangers in the national parks have told the tourists there's no camping," I said.

"Right," said Nell. "And the lake is as low as it's ever been. Anyone can see that. But don't talk now."

I hadn't opened my eyes, but before I could see anything wrong with the woods before me, I could smell it: the acrid scent of burning brush. Then I could hear it, too. The exploding of sap in the tiny branches, the distant crack of big limbs grown too heavy for the trees as the fire burned them halfway through, and the crash they made as they fell to the forest floor.

"No!"

"Keep your eyes closed," said Nell. This time she said it, or I wouldn't have done it. I didn't want to know what might burn next.

Because the hill upon which the lodge sat was steep, coming up from the lake you couldn't see the building itself until you were almost there. It was the same with the cabins on the rise behind the lodge, one of which we'd stayed in our first summer there. You couldn't see the cabins until you were almost up to the road.

What I saw this time, with my eyes still closed, was gray smoke curling off the roofs of two of the cabins, where cinders from the woods behind them had blown across the shingles.

Nell pulled my hand closer and squeezed it. "Everybody's okay," she said. "It's the middle of the afternoon. Nobody's in any of the cabins now."

Even as she said it, the roof of one of the cabins shimmered in the heat. Then, as if somebody inside had turned on a lamp, it began to glow orange at the windows and through the screen door. I knew, whether I kept on looking or not, that in a moment it would be gone.

"We're not staying in those cabins this time," I said.

"No," said Nell. "You're in number eleven, up the hill to the other side of the lodge. I know."

"Does eleven burn?"

She didn't have to answer. I could see that the fire hadn't moved that way, and wouldn't. The wind had pushed it over the grass in front of the older cabins and across the road, toward the woods that separated the lodge from the lake, rather than further up the hill or across the slope to the lodge itself. There was a wide swath of black over the grass that had been brown. It was the trees at the upper edge of the woods, where the path to the lake started to get steep and stumbly over the roots, that I'd heard crackling.

"Thank goodness," I said. "If Kip's stuffed animals burned, she'd whine all the way home."

"No, she wouldn't," Nell said quietly. "She's older than that now, too."

I opened my eyes. The moon didn't seem to have moved a bit. Nell hadn't moved, either.

"I'm just happy that the fortuneteller at the fair didn't want my two dollars if she was going to show me something like that," I said. "Is there really going to be a fire?"

Nell shrugged. "You saw what you saw," she said.

"What else can you show me?"

Nell looked surprised, but only for a moment. "I guess I wasn't paying attention," she said. "Why don't you relax for a minute here, and think about what you know."

"Are you a teacher or a fortuneteller?" I asked her.

"Are all your teachers in school?"

"Are you here tonight to show me that the lodge won't be here forever?"

"If you weren't here and a tree fell in the forest — never mind a tree that had burst into flames and black smoke and littered the ground with chattering squirrels whose tails were singed — just a tree — if it fell and you weren't here, would it be here, whole and green, when you came back?" I didn't know. And I did. But I wanted her to say it. Or I didn't. So I asked her something else and hoped maybe we'd get back to it.

"Now that I've held your hand," I said, "will I see what's going to happen again?"

"Now you know, with the certainty of the smell of smoke, that what you count on can be gone in minutes, and you have to keep growing past it into something you have to learn each new day or miss entirely, and you ask me if you'll see what's going to happen *again?*"

"You mean I already know?"

"What else do you want to know?"

I was afraid to think very hard for the answer. I didn't want to see another fire, didn't want to smell wood smoke or see the orange, flickering light behind the windows of places I knew.

"Will I get married?"

"Isn't that a question unworthy of you?"

"It isn't simple? Yes or no?"

"What if I say yes? What if, when you're fifteen, just around the corner from now, armed with my 'yes,' you meet some Jimmy the Monkey in a black T-shirt with the sleeves rolled up and motorcycle boots? He says 'Why not?' and you figure, 'The fortuneteller *said* I was gonna get married, so this must be the way to go.' What if that?"

"You couldn't tell me how *old* I'd be when I got married?"

"What if six Jimmy the Monkeys asked you, all when you were twenty-three?"

"What if you told me which number I'd accept?"

"How would you count it if one of them asked you twice? Once on his knees in the mud and the second time with a note in a bottle that he'd pitched off an outbound tanker after he went to sea with a broken heart because you only said 'Maybe' the first time, seeing as how you weren't sure which number the fortuneteller meant?"

She was good at this. I sat back in my straight chair. "When will the fire be?"

"The woods burn all the time, everywhere."

"These woods?"

"Not tonight," Nell said. "Not tomorrow. And sometimes it's not a fire at all. That's all you need to know."

"This isn't like a genie thing, is it?" I asked. "You don't have to tell me anything."

"I think I've already told you quite a lot," she said.

I thought about what I knew. The question about getting married was an old one with me and Kip and our friends. We used the numbers on dollar bills to predict when we'd marry, how many children we'd have, and what their names would be. We used playing cards, too, and dice, and we'd been talking about it since before we knew what it meant. Once, while

Mom was driving us somewhere, Kip had taken her thumb out of her mouth and turned to me in the back seat.

"When you grow up," she asked solemnly, "are you gonna have a husband?"

"Probably," I said.

"You gonna have sax with him?"

She'd asked it coolly, without humor, matter-of-factly. Then she'd popped her thumb back into her mouth.

In the driver's seat, Mom didn't get it at first. Then she did, and I've wondered lots of times since then how she held the car on the road.

"Your sister doesn't suck her thumb anymore," Nell said.

"No," I said, and then, "Stop that!"

"Sorry. It's been a while since anybody's been out to this neck of the woods, and I'm as curious as the next fortuneteller."

"You don't get many visitors?"

"Not as many as you might think, given what fun it is to visit a fortuneteller."

I had wondered. There didn't seem to be anybody visiting the circus that night but me. Acrobats, freaks, tumblers, dwarves, tigers — and a tiger handler somewhere, I supposed, and Nell, of course, but nobody else who'd come through the woods for the show.

"Some nights it's busier than others." said Nell. "But people don't come out here in groups or pairs, even on the warmest nights when the moon's brightest and nobody can sleep much because it's prettier outside than it is in their dreams."

"Was I led here?"

Nell smiled. "You might have stayed in bed and listened to the loons," she said. "You could have convinced yourself that the calliope music was somebody's radio on a boat out on the lake, so far away that the night or the woods had bent the sound into something new and strange. You might have stayed in bed and listened. Or you might have gone back to sleep." She drew herself up out of the chair and walked around the table. She stood behind me and put her hands on my shoulders. They felt strong and sure, and I thought, *a healer's hands,* though I didn't know why. "You might have told Antoinette you didn't want to go any further when you passed the big sign for 'Nature's Mistakes.' Some imagine the worst and just want to go back home. Or, when Antoinette sat you down so she could show off on the high wire for you, you might have stayed put, assumed she was your special friend, and that was that."

"Was I meant to?"

Nell shrugged. "You might have stayed to flirt with Jimmy the Monkey," she said. "He'd have liked that. He'd have climbed out of the pyramid again and brought it down around his ears to give you a laugh. He's done it before."

"I wasn't supposed to follow the tiger?"

"The tiger was just being a tiger," Nell said. "Following the tiger was one way to go."

"I wouldn't have seen your lantern in the woods."

"You might have followed anything. Fireflies. Your nose. But I'm awfully glad you found your way here. I'll give that tiger a treat when he happens by again, just in case it *was* his idea."

I knew that she was playing with me, but, even while I was still beside her, while her hands were still on my shoulders, I felt that I was fortunate. I could imagine that if I told my friends about Nell, they'd call me a goof for not asking her more questions, thinking she might let slip something that would make them giggle and squeal. Would I be rich and live in a house on a hill? Would I ever visit Africa or India? It was a fun game to play, but Nell was right. How much future would anybody really want to know?

My mother used to tell us a story of her brother's pet duck. He'd gotten it for Christmas or a birthday when he was just a little boy, seven or eight, I can't remember. The duck was little, too. It waddled and wandered around for a while, looking this way and that at the new world with which it had been presented, quacking experimentally, making everyone in the family laugh. Then it turned left when it might have turned right, got itself stuck in the hedge that still borders my grandmother's yard, and broke its neck. An hour after it had climbed out of its little box, it was dead. Mom couldn't even remember whether her brother had given it a name.

If people could know the future, who'd ever give a little boy a duck?

NINE

NELL'S HANDS WERE GENTLE AS WELL AS STRONG ON MY shoulders, and I must have been exhausted. I went to sleep right in that straight-backed chair. I don't remember dreaming. When I woke, I was still upright, but I wasn't stiff or sore. Instead I felt rested and secure. I opened my eyes easily and looked across the wagon without surprise. Nell was sitting in the other chair. Her head was bowed a little, and at first I thought that she'd fallen asleep, too, but she hadn't. In the light of the single lantern, she was knitting.

On the table between us there was a blue paper plate with a sandwich on it. Beside it was a mug full of milk. I realized I was hungry.

"Ham and swiss cheese on rye with mayo," said Nell. "Your favorite? Yes, I thought so."

The sandwich was perfect, and the milk was wonderfully cold.

When I'd finished, I looked across the table at Nell. "It's time to go, isn't it?"

"Come in, Antoinette," Nell said, and I heard Toni on the wagon's steps. A moment later she peered around the corner at me and smiled.

I looked at Nell. "Can I come back?"

"Whenever you want," she said. "For a while." Then she turned back to Toni, who was still standing by the door. "What have you got to be shy about? Your future's no mystery anymore, is it?"

"No, ma'am," Toni said, but she stayed at the door.

"Oh, never mind," Nell said. "Just show Molly the way back, Antoinette."

"Thank you," I said.

Nell looked surprised for a moment, then she smiled. "A pleasure making your acquaintance," she said.

Outside it was as dark as it had been when I'd found my way to the wagon. With Toni leading the way, we were off in a direction that I would have said was precisely wrong.

"Did Nell summon you to do this or something?" I asked her. "How did you know to come for me?"

"It could have been Jimmy," Toni said. She giggled. "Would you have liked that better?"

"Nell doesn't seem to think much of Jimmy."

"Nell's an old lady," Toni whispered. "It's kind of weird. She was already an old lady when she —" Toni cut herself off.

"What?" I asked.

"Nothing," Toni said. "Just, she's an old lady. That's all.

What would she know about Jimmy? Or sailing across the tent on a trapeze, for that matter? Or balancing over everybody on a high wire? Or dancing in the woods when the fire's only embers and the sun's in a hurry to return?"

She stopped on the path so abruptly that I almost stepped on her heel. She pointed to the left a little, where there seemed to be no path at all, only thick woods so dark that even the bright moonlight by which we'd been walking couldn't get through.

"You go that way," she said.

"Are you sure?"

"Straight through there."

"Will I see you again some night?"

"What Nell said," Toni shrugged. "I guess that's up to you."

I don't know why I wasn't ready to walk away from her then. I did know, without asking, that she wouldn't come with me, or that she couldn't, not even if I told her that in the living room of the cabin there was a comfy old sofa where she could sleep, or that we could squeeze a cot into the second bedroom and she could sleep with me.

"Do you see us there?" I asked her, pointing into the patch of woods she indicated as my way home.

Toni shook her head. "Just when you come looking for me," she said. "For us."

"How long have you been here?"

Toni laughed. "All that time with Nell in her wagon and you're still full of questions. What did you two do? Just sit and drink tea?"

She must have seen that I was reluctant to go on by myself, but there would be no more answers that night.

"Through these woods, you said?"

"Believe it or not," she said.

"I can't see any way through. There's no path."

"You'll find your way out, same as you found your way in," Toni said. "This time, anyway." Then she turned her own way, which might have been back the same way we'd come.

"See you," I said.

"Not for long," she whispered, and she was gone.

I took a step into the thick woods Toni had indicated, and then another. There was no mysterious path opening up before me. Thorns scratched my arms and vines grabbed at my ankles. I couldn't see how even squirrels or chipmunks could get through this thicket, but Toni wouldn't have pointed me in the wrong direction, surely, and she knew where I was trying to go. I pushed ahead, protecting my face with my hands so the branches wouldn't slap me, sometimes kicking at the snarled and tangled underbrush to make room for the next step.

It had been a cool night, but now I could feel the sweat on my forehead and my back. I told myself it was the hard work of breaking through the woods and not fear that I was headed nowhere. I must have told myself that out loud, because a moment later a voice answered me.

"Molly?"

It was Dad.

"I'm here," I said. Then I saw the wavering beam of a flashlight. I couldn't tell how far away it was, but he hadn't been shouting when he'd said my name, so it couldn't have been far.

"Molly?"

"Here," I said, and then the flashlight found me and my dad crashed impatiently through the dark woods.

"Thank God," he said. "Are you all right?"

All right? Maybe I was. Or maybe I was as crazy as one of those people who hear voices that aren't there or see people nobody else can see. I started asking myself that the next day, after I'd slept like a rock through what was left of the night and eaten blueberry pancakes on the porch. Mom and Dad sipped their coffee and looked at each other, wondering, I guess, how much to ask me. Kip chattered as she usually did, pointing out that it was cloudy, and asking if we could go to the movies that afternoon if it wasn't a beach day, and then saying "please" three or four times very dramatically before either Mom or Dad had time to answer yes or no.

Over the coffee and exchanged looks they decided not to push it. That didn't surprise me, and it doesn't now. From their standpoint I'd been gone — what? An hour? Mom had looked in late at night because Kip had been coughing a little in her sleep. When she'd found my bed empty, she'd woken Dad and he'd taken the flashlight and headed for the lake, assuming I'd gone down that path to see the stars shining off the water. It was on the way back up from the lake that he'd heard me stumbling through the woods. He didn't know how long I'd been up and out, and I couldn't tell him, because I didn't know either. It felt like a long time and a lot of ground covered, but what could I compare it to? How much time did it normally take to make the acquaintance of a trapeze artist and follow a tiger to the wagon of a fortune-teller who would toss your questions back at you and then feed you ham and cheese on rye?

If Dad had made it back to the cabin without running into me, he and Mom might have gone for help and the night would have expanded into an adventure for them, too. As it was, Mom had woken up and I was gone. Maybe I'd been out of bed for just a few minutes. Less than half an hour later, Dad was back with me in tow. Once they were sure I wasn't hurt or frightened, they only told me I'd scared them by taking off into the woods at night and shouldn't do it again, no matter how sweet the night air or how brightly the moon seemed to light up the path behind the cabin.

After breakfast, as if it were any day, Kip and I left the table together and walked around the back of the lodge to meet with Snow. We must have eaten early that morning. There was nobody else climbing up the slope to the playhouse, though the door was open, and from the hill we could hear Snow thumping around inside.

By then I'd reached the point where I knew what to do as Snow's helper without being told. I collected lanyard strings and cut them into the proper length, or made sure the little tin trays had enough paint of each color so nobody would feel she didn't have choices. I even guessed with Snow how many kids might show up on a given morning, and I reminded her sometimes what we'd already done that week. Some mornings I'd have fifteen minutes with her before anyone else came in, because if Kip and I got there first, as we did on that day, Kip usually played outside in the sand or on the rope swing until some of the other kids showed up. She liked to be surprised as much as any of them did, and listening to Snow make plans with me as we distributed paint brushes or counted out glass beads spoiled some of the anticipation, I guess.

But on this day Kip rushed up the hill as soon as she saw the door was open. She beat me to the playhouse by several strides, and I could hear her talking to Snow before I even reached the steps.

". . . and nobody knew where she was," I heard her say. "We don't even know if *she* knows where she was!"

The floor of the playhouse creaked as I stepped in out of the sunlight. Snow looked up from the table, where she was spreading out sheets of cardboard. Her eyes met mine as if Kip wasn't there. I don't know what she saw in mine. I think I saw recognition in hers.

After a moment, Kip broke the spell by asking what we were going to do that day.

"We're going to make maps," Snow said. "It's so we can find our way through the woods the same way we'd follow the road into town."

"To get ice cream after dinner!" Kip shouted.

"Ice cream after dinner, or any number of other delights," Snow said. "Although not all of them will be on the maps we'll make, will they, Molly?"

As soon as there was an opportunity, I'd talk to her about the circus, of course. But not with Kip there. And before long the rest of the kids came in, too, so there was no opportunity to say much more than "How many of these do you need?," "What colors do you want?," or "You'll see your mom and dad at lunchtime, I promise. And think how much they'll like this watercolor of the lake you're painting, if you'll only stop crying into the blue, because you're washing it out so that it will look like clouds, see?"

Several times during the morning I caught Snow looking at me, or I thought I did. She seemed less anxious than I was to have the conversation I knew we would have. When lunchtime finally came, I helped her make sure that each camper had the right map, the right painting, the right beaded keychain, the right sweater or sweatshirt, and the right socks, too, because Kip had taken off her sneakers and socks and suggested that they all mix theirs up in a pile in the middle of the floor. By the time I'd finished and had the last camper out the door, Snow had gathered up her own things.

"Don't be late for lunch," she said, because Kip had run ahead. "You'll worry your parents again. They must have been frantic last night." That wasn't what I wanted to talk to Snow about. I wanted to find out what she knew about the circus and Toni and Nell.

But she said she had no time. "I've got to run errands on my way home" is what she told me.

I nodded, though Snow and errands didn't seem to fit. Errands were for busy parents checking their watches as they wrenched their minivans out of too-tight spaces in the grocery store parking lot and tried to calculate whether they could get across town to the dry cleaner and stop at the bank before the school bus dropped the first kid at home. Snow had no children. Why should she have errands? I don't think she even had a watch.

"You're in a hurry?" I asked her.

"I'm giving piano lessons this afternoon," she said.

That seemed inconceivable, too. Snow scolding some kid with dirty fingernails because she hadn't practiced her etudes? I could see her giving tambourine lessons, having first taught her pupil to make the tambourine, but not piano.

"We'll talk tomorrow, Molly. Or the day after that. How much longer is your family staying?"

I'd never known Snow to sound so much like most adults: a mom, or a math teacher, or the woman in the gift shop who was afraid you'd break something if you played with it on the floor but tried to keep the worry out of her voice.

"A few more days," I said.

TEN

BACK WHEN WE FIRST STARTED COMING TO THE LODGE, dinner was the hardest time. The waitresses were local girls, home from college or home forever, and there weren't enough of them. The service was slow on a good night, and on a night when a big family reunion was in progress around the long table at the far end of the dining room or out on the porch under the stars, it could stop altogether.

The first several times Kip and I would jump up from the table to run and throw Ping-Pong balls around the game room or slide down the hill on the plastic cars or race up to Snow's playhouse to see our own clay figures drying inside on the cluttered table, we'd ask permission. After that, we'd just go. We'd run until Mom or Dad had told us three or four times to stop running in the dining room. Then we'd walk very quickly, elbows churning, much more likely to knock somebody's coffee in his lap than if we'd been running.

Each excursion would last less time as we wore out more

of the alternatives to sitting and waiting for our dinner. Each time we raced back to the table, we'd crane our necks and sniff loudly, pretending that we were trying to smell whether the food had arrived. When it still wasn't there, Kip and I would clutch our stomachs and stagger the last few steps to our chairs, as if we barely had the strength to reach the table and would certainly require assistance lifting the fork or spoon if anybody ever did show up with the food.

It drove Dad crazy, and it drove Mom crazier. More than once at dinnertime they decided that we wouldn't come back to the lodge again, but we always did. Each winter, when it was time to make a reservation, they must have forgotten the dinners.

Anyway, by this particular summer, the days of racing in and out of the dining room had passed. Kip might have still done it if I was leading the way or willing to follow, but I wasn't, and she took her cue from me. So that night, when Dad asked me not to sing at the table and I started humming just loudly enough for Kip alone to hear me, she hummed back. And of course when she hummed, she was louder, and Dad heard her, too. Then when he turned to tell her to stop being a smart aleck, I raised my eyebrows and frowned to imitate him. It must have been an acceptable likeness. Kip, who had just taken a mouthful of milk, sputtered and shook until it ran out her nose.

"Kip, that's gross," I said, probably loudly enough to alert several tables full of diners, who'd otherwise have missed the show.

"Damn," Dad said.

Kip kicked at me under the table and grazed my leg.

"Ow! Dad, she kicked me!"

"It's your fault," Kip hissed. "You made me laugh."

I had, and I was old enough to know better, as Mom and Dad told me often. (Old enough to walk away into the woods in pursuit of the circus, too, and to have my fortune told, after a fashion, though we hadn't talked about that.)

After we'd arrived back at the cabin and I'd been sent to one room and Kip to another following more shouting, recriminations, and — this was rare, actually — an exchange of punches, Mom tried to talk with me.

"What's up?" she asked, assuming, I guess, that something had me frightened. She didn't know the half of it, and I wasn't telling her. "Is this about being out in the woods? Are you just now figuring out you were scared we wouldn't find you? We did, honey. We always will."

It was loving reassurance sincerely offered, and on lots of other occasions it had worked, but in a moment that night I knew it would never quite work again. I knew it with a clarity as bright as circus lights, constant as the undertone of the calliope, sly as a fortuneteller's promise. They would love me, and they would miss me when I was gone, but they would not entirely find me, ever again, unless for a moment or an hour or a day I wanted to be found. The woods would burn, one way or another. I'd find myself, if I could.

A little later, Kip came in. We started playing Scrabble, and eventually Mom and Dad drifted in, too, he to help Kip, she to urge him to stay out of the game. We usually played until one of us started making words like *glorp* and *frix*, always trying to keep a straight face while offering some half-plausible definition.

This time the game ended differently. While the score was still close and Dad was denying that he'd tipped the balance by showing Kip *quark* and trying to explain what it meant, I discovered *moon* on my little rack of letters and put it down in front of *glow,* which was already on the board. It wasn't a lot of points, but it stopped the game.

The stars always seemed closer and brighter in Vermont. Somebody had told us it was because at home there was so much artificial light shining up from the city that the night sky seemed less impressive. Maybe that was it, or maybe we were just more likely to look up when we were on vacation.

That night, we all looked up. I could see every summer constellation. I could recognize Cassiopeia, the two dippers, and a few others, but the sky was so thoroughly studded with stars on that clear night it seemed silly to think of them in small groups with names. Renegade stars blinked and shimmered mischievously in the margins of the shapes of hunters, bears, and lopsided dogs. The sky that night was not about recognizing and labeling. It was about riot and profusion. It was more stars than any science teacher could name in ten lifetimes. That night sky mocked charts and might have reminded us that the naming had begun with fear and worship, if we'd been inclined to think that way that night.

We weren't. We just sat on my bed and looked out the window. Even Kip was quiet. And after a while, still without a word, she scooted over and hugged me with her blond head — blonder than mine — to my chest, as the moon hovered over us and appeared not to move at all.

"It looks like an apple," Kip said. "Like in the poem Dad told us."

For a moment none of us knew what she meant, and then Mom and Dad and I did, all at once.

"The Yeats poem," I said.

"Go ahead, you old ham," Mom said. "Recite it again."

Dad had some poetry from memory, and under the moon that night, he did recite the sad one called "The Song of the Wandering Aengus," which he said he'd memorized back when he was not much older than I. In a soft and even voice, he said the words an Irish poet named William Butler Yeats had written a long time ago in another country, under the same moon and stars.

> I went out to the hazel wood,
> Because a fire was in my head,
> And cut and peeled a hazel wand,
> And hooked a berry to a thread,
> And when white moths were on the wing,
> And moth-like stars were flickering out,
> I dropped a berry in a stream
> And caught a little silver trout.

When I had laid it on the floor
I went to blow the fire a-flame,
But something rustled on the floor,
And someone called me by my name:
It had become a glimmering girl
With apple blossoms in her hair
Who called me by my name and ran
And faded through the brightening air.

Though I am old with wandering
Through hollow lands and hilly lands,
I will find out where she has gone,
And kiss her lips and take her hands;
And walk among long dappled grass,
And pluck till time and times are done,
The silver apples of the moon,
The golden apples of the sun.

Usually, when anybody said anything for as long as it took
Dad to recite the poem, Kip jumped in at the end with her
own story, or at least a list of questions: "What's a hollow
land?" she might have said, or "Who was Hazel Wood?"

But on this night, she sat silently with the rest of us. Together we just looked out the window at the sky. And maybe,
for a time, there was as much wonder in that room as there
ever was in the woods.

ELEVEN

THAT NIGHT I SLEPT LIKE A STONE AGAIN, AND WHEN KIP pawed me awake in the morning, pretending to be a cat who wanted company, I didn't remember any dreams. I'd slept so well that in that moment of waking I wasn't sure that what had happened in the woods hadn't been a dream.

But it hadn't, of course, and I knew that before I brushed my teeth, and even before I told Kip to stop pawing at me and going on about how kittens needed pancakes.

It was a cool morning, a reminder that fall would follow summer everywhere, though it would happen a lot earlier here in the mountains than it would at home. We all padded around the cabin in sweatshirts for the first little while that we were awake and wondered whether it would get warm enough to swim that day, though we all knew it would.

We ate on the porch. Our waitress was Virginia, my favorite that summer. She had short dark hair, enormous brown eyes, and a stud through her tongue that she would show you by waggling it, if you asked. Or at least she would if you were a kid.

We'd all taken off our sweatshirts before she brought the coffee and tea.

"She doesn't look much older than you are," Mom had said the first time Virginia had asked us what we wanted. "Maybe one summer you'll get a job waitressing here at the lodge."

"If you do, will you get your tongue pierced?" Kip wanted to know.

"Ugh," Dad said. "Why would anybody want to do that?"

It seemed as awful to me as it did to him, but I didn't say so.

"Kip's the one more likely to get her tongue pierced," Mom said. "And her bellybutton. She's also the one more likely to get a tattoo."

"I don't think so," Kip said. "Yuck."

That afternoon, Virginia laughed when I told her about Kip's reaction to Mom's guess. I'd gone into the kitchen for a glass of water, and she'd surprised me. She was after an apple, and she found one and asked me if I wanted one, too. I didn't, but I said I did, and we sat down at the big kitchen table, just the two of us.

"I remember when I felt the same way Kip does," Virginia said.

"Why'd you do it, then?"

She shrugged. She couldn't tell me, or wouldn't. I was still only a kid.

"What did your parents say?"

113

"Mom wasn't real pleased," Virginia said. "But it's not like it's the only thing she has to worry about. She's still got four kids at home younger than me — and one of them is my half-bright sister with two bad legs — and my two half brothers drive her nuts. She had to get a restraining order against one of them — my older brother, Buddy — because he'd come around the house when nobody was there and steal whatever he could carry. Stole the TV set the first time, then came back for the VCR. That's why I got this job, I bet. Mary and Brett, who own this place, they feel bad for me, coming from that sorry family. A lot of people in town do, except for the ones whose families are as screwed up as mine."

I'd heard about restraining orders from television, but I'd never known anybody in real life who'd had anything to do with one. That and the stud in her tongue and the tattoo she probably had but hadn't shown me yet made Virginia a pretty exciting presence in my summer. She was what she was, and I was the only member of my family who knew it. Mom and Dad probably thought she was college-bound, never mind her tongue.

"Is it a good job?"

"Not if you don't have to take it," she said. "Waitressing's waitressing, wherever you do it. But maybe it's better than a lot of places, I guess. It's close. I only live on the next hill over. Even if I oversleep, I can cut through the woods and be here in twenty minutes. I can fix my hair on the way. I've done it lots of times."

So I had to ask her, but she said no.

"What kind of music?" she asked.

"Calliope."

"I don't know what that is."

"It's like what you hear at the circus. Kind of tooting and whistling. I don't know where else you'd hear it."

"I did go to a circus once," Virginia said. "I couldn't believe it came all the way up here to the sticks. It must have made a wrong turn after Burlington and got lost." She laughed. "All of it. The lions and tigers and elephants, too. Or just one elephant, actually, and he looked like an old one."

"Was there a fortuneteller?" I was still hoping for company.

"I don't think so," she said. "Not that I saw, anyway. Just the usual animals, and a woman who rode a horse bareback around a ring. A woman whose best days in spandex and lycra were behind her, which you could see if you got up close to where she was riding. Stuff like that."

Virginia took a bite from the apple and thought about the circus some more. "They had popcorn and cotton candy, and those syrupy things, you know, with the crushed ice in the paper cup. I remember those empty cones were everywhere in the parking lot the next day, and they were blowing all over town in the wind for a couple days after that."

"It was in town?"

"Sure," she said. "In the field right across from the school. Only place flat enough to set up that big tent, I guess."

So it hadn't even been in the woods. I might have left it at that, but I didn't.

"Was it just you who went? Or did you go with your family?"

"We all went. Or everybody who was home. It wasn't much, but it was a big deal for around here. So Mom went, and the kids."

"How old is your sister?" I asked.

"Toni?" she asked. "Thirteen. About the same as you, right?"

"Right," I said. "Toni?"

"Short for Antoinette."

"I know," I said.

Virginia had finished her apple in a couple of bites. Now she got up. "Toni went to the circus, too. And she smiled all the time she was there, even though, like I said, there wasn't that much to it. No calapoly, or whatever you called it. Just a scratchy soundtrack from the loudspeaker on one of the trucks, and a couple of clowns running around blowing plastic horns." She wiped her hands on her jeans. "But it was okay, you know? Better than going out to see a movie you really don't want to see except that somebody's asked you and he's got a car and there's nothing on TV."

So that left Snow, and the next day gave me the chance to corner her. It rained all morning, so we couldn't leave the playhouse, and the little kids made a mess. A big mess. By lunchtime, every board game Snow had was spread out on one of the wooden tables or the floor. Little plastic tokens and red and white dice had rolled under the benches and into the corners, and there were scraps of crepe paper and ribbon all over the place, and strips of newspaper that had never made it into papier-mâché, and play money from a Monopoly game that was kept in a big brown envelope because the box was long gone.

At noon everybody scattered, and I grabbed Kip. I told her I was going to help Snow clean up, so she should tell Mom and Dad I'd be late. Kip was hungry enough not to argue about having to walk to our cabin by herself. Besides that, she was in a hurry to line up at the playhouse door. Snow had this huge collection of beat up umbrellas, which she lent out when it rained as long as you brought them back the next morning. Kip wanted the one with the Winnie the Pooh characters on it, which you could usually get only by being first in line, or second, if the person who was first wanted the Star Wars umbrella.

I started picking things up off the floor even before the final kid had left, waving the last, most woebegone umbrella, and splashing across the little rivers the rain had made through the pine needles.

The rain hadn't let up while I was collecting game pieces and sorting them into the right packages, or while I was separating the bits of paper and cloth that could still be used for collages from what we'd finally throw out, or while Snow swept the sand and dust into a pile beside the open screen door. The temperature had dropped with the rain, and I wished I'd taken Mom's advice and brought a jacket.

Snow looked out at the rain and said, "What do you do with the afternoon in this weather?"

117

"Play cards, sometimes," I said. "Or Scrabble. What do they do in the woods?" I was hoping she wouldn't ask, "Who?"

"They get wet," Snow said. She still wasn't looking at me. She seemed to be trying to decide whether to say anything more. I don't know why I waited for her, but I did, and after a while she said, "You didn't think it was a dream or something? The first time?"

"The first time was during the day," I said. "In the afternoon. And all I saw was Toni. It was only for a second, and then she was gone, so I wasn't sure what I'd seen, but I knew I hadn't been dreaming."

"People have daydreams," Snow said. "Sometimes somebody who's seen Toni or heard the calliope even a couple of times will convince herself it's music from a dance somewhere across the lake. They rub their eyes and say what they saw was shadows, or the sunlight through the trees."

"But the second time was at night," I said.

"I know," Snow nodded. "You can't wish it away now."

She was looking at me. Her brown eyes were steady. "I'm sorry I avoided you before," she said.

"Piano lessons," I said. "Right."

"Oh, I give piano lessons." I smiled and Snow raised her eyebrows. "You find that hard to believe? I give skiing lessons in the winter, too."

"Yeah," I said. "Skiing I can see. And water-skiing in the summer?"

"They stopped that here after a little boy got hurt," she said. "But you didn't stay behind to talk about me."

118

"Why would I want to wish it away?"

But I knew, even as I asked.

As she sat looking out at the rain, she sighed, and her shoulders looked heavy. "Almost everybody who sees the circus eventually forgets almost everything they've seen," she said. "I said 'wish it away,' but that's not always it. There's some wishing sometimes, but other times maybe it just happens, kind of like doing yourself a favor."

"Because you wish you hadn't found it?"

"Not exactly," Snow said. She was looking at me now, instead of the rain. "Think about it. You've known for a long time that you won't always be a little girl. You've played games with your sister that you really don't want to play anymore."

I looked at Snow and beyond her. I remembered something that had happened two Christmases ago. We'd hauled the boxes of lights and decorations out of the cellar, and Mom, Dad, Kip, and I were rooting through them, trying to decide where to put the cardboard Santas and green paper wreaths that Kip and I had been making and bringing home since nursery school. Mom had saved even the faded ones, and the ones with just dried spots of paste where there had been cutouts of ornaments or flowers.

We decorated the house for Halloween, of course, and for Easter, too, but that was nothing compared to what we did for Christmas. Some years there wasn't a downstairs window without a Santa, a wreath, or a sleigh full of stick figure children drawn by stick figure reindeer.

On this particular day of Christmas decorating, when Kip turned up our stockings, she clamored for the game she was certain we would play. We'd each take up our stockings, cram them with the toys that we already had — old stuffed animals, dog-eared paperbacks, ornaments that had fallen off the tree — and then pour everything out on the floor, pretending total surprise and wild delight. I'm sure I invented the game for Kip on her second or third Christmas, and it must have felt as much a part of the season as a turkey dinner, hoping for a snowstorm, and Santa Claus himself. But on this particular afternoon, surrounded by the glorious clutter of Christmases past, I wouldn't play.

"Come on," Kip said. "It's the stocking game. We always play it. Every Christmas."

"I don't want to," I told her. When she asked why, I shrugged. Maybe I couldn't have told her.

Kip was impossibly good-natured, even at an age when kids aren't. She pretty quickly took my declaration in stride and began suggesting other games we might play. When I said I just wanted to look at what else was in the boxes, she furrowed her brow for a moment, then nodded and said that's what she wanted to do, too. We returned to unpacking.

While Kip was redeeming the moment that could have poisoned Christmas if she'd let it, I looked over at Mom. She looked as if she was about to cry. When she knew I'd caught her, she looked away.

Snow was right. I'd played games with my sister that I didn't really want to play anymore. But I'd also stopped playing some of the games that she'd happily have kept playing. I'd convinced her that half the TV shows she liked were "baby shows" so that she'd agree to watch the programs I liked instead. I'd done what big sisters do.

"So when Kip finds the circus and comes to me to talk about it, I'll tell her I'm not interested?"

Snow shook her head. "Who knows?" she said. "How many kids find the circus? Did you see any of the other kids who are staying at the lodge when you were there?"

It had been just me, and I told her so.

"You don't know," she said.

"But *you* must." Snow had been at the lodge forever. Hundreds and hundreds of kids had passed through the playhouse. Lots of them must have been led to the circus as I had been, or gone out looking for it, or stumbled over it — whatever had happened.

"I'll tell you a story," Snow said. "A long time ago, I was a teacher. I worked in a boarding school. Just girls." She smiled to remember it. "I was just a girl, too, but besides being a teacher, I was a house mistress. That meant I had a room in one of the dormitories where the girls lived. I ate three meals a day with them. I helped them with their homework in the evenings. Some of them were homesick, and they'd cry on my shoulder.

"One night at about eleven o'clock, there was a soft knock at my door. I'd gone to bed, but I wasn't asleep. It was one of the younger girls in the house, a girl named Gretchen. She was short and thin, not very good at sports. She was left out of a lot of things, I guess. She had gray eyes that were almost no color at all, and you could see traces of veins in her eyelids and in her neck, as if they were too close to the surface. She looked fragile.

"I don't think she'd ever spoken a dozen words at a time to me, but she sat down on my old couch and began to talk. She was afraid of her mother, who expected her to be smart and popular. She rarely saw her father, who traveled all the time, but she described him in great detail — down to the tips of his manicured fingers. She was lost in algebra and behind in Spanish. She told me she'd been thinking about killing herself."

I couldn't help smiling.

"I know," said Snow. "It doesn't sound like a very good reason for suicide, does it? But Gretchen sat on that old, beat-up couch and told me that hanging was no good, because she was such a klutz that she was sure any knot she made would slip and she'd just crash to the floor and wake everybody up. For the same reason, she didn't want to shoot herself: she might miss, too much noise, and, besides, who'd sell her a gun? She'd thought about cutting her wrists, too, but she was afraid of the pain. So pills was the only way it could be, once she could steal enough of them from somebody and work up the nerve."

Snow paused. "It had been a rainy day," she said. "Like today. In the rain, the school could be a gloomy place. I can remember walking down the corridor on a gray afternoon, hearing the same sad songs on a dozen different portable stereos.

"But Gretchen wasn't just indulging her melancholy, or at least that's how it seemed to me. She was talking about suicide like somebody who'd done her homework, and I was frightened. I hadn't heard the nickel wisdom about how people who talk about suicide never do it.

"So I sat and listened to her all night long. Maybe I'd have done that even if I'd been older and wiser."

"What happened to her?" I asked. "Did she kill herself? Did you send her to a psychiatrist?"

"She talked until sunup and beyond," Snow said. "She hardly repeated herself. It turned out she was quite a talker, if somebody would sit still and listen. Then suddenly she stopped in the middle of a sentence and asked me what time it was."

"What?" I said.

"That's right." Snow nodded. "'What time is it?' I looked at my watch and told her it was ten minutes after seven. I'd been listening to her for a little over eight hours. I was so tired I couldn't see straight, but I was sure I'd done the right thing. I'd helped her through the darkest night."

"Was she grateful, at least?"

Snow smiled. "Sometimes you can't count on that," she said. "After I told her it was ten minutes after seven, she leapt off my couch and said, 'Oh my God! I've got to pick up my books and get some breakfast or I'm gonna be late for English class!'"

"She just left?"

"On the run," Snow said.

"Did she come back another night?"

"Never did. I'd see her in the dormitory, of course. Pass her on the stairs or run into her at lunch. She was always pleasant, but we never had another conversation that was anything other than small talk. I think that night made a bigger impression on me than it did on her."

It was still raining hard, but it was also getting to the point where, if Mom and Dad and Kip were waiting for me to eat their lunch, they'd be figuring they'd waited long enough. Any picture Dad had planned of the girls returning from a morning at camp would only have had one girl in it, and maybe they'd even be wondering if I'd gone into the woods again. But this conversation wasn't finished just because Snow's story was over, though I thought I knew why she'd told it to me.

"So you think that's the way it is with some kids who find the circus? It's just there until they find out what time it is and remember where they're supposed to be?"

"Something like that," Snow said.

"You think I'll forget what I saw? Forget Toni and Nell?"

Snow smiled. "And Jimmy the Monkey?"

"Him, too," I said. "You think I'll ask somebody the time and realize I'm late and forget what I've seen?"

"No, I don't," she said. "I think you'll go on growing up, but somewhere you'll remember what happened along the way. More than that. Keep something of it with you."

"Something of what?"

"You know how you meet some people, some adults, and you just can't imagine that they were ever children?"

I did. I thought of the lunch lady at school. She was no taller than some of the tallest girls in the sixth grade, but she seemed to have been born middle-aged. She shouted at us all the time, and she began each shout by barking "People! People!" I liked it better when somebody screamed "Boys and girls!"

When I'd told Snow about the lunch lady, she said, "You won't be like that."

But that was only the smallest part of it, and I was sure of it even then. I knew I'd go back into the woods to find the circus again, and I knew that whatever I found, I'd never forget. Already I could hear the twigs break as I chased Toni's shadow the first time I saw her. I could smell the rain on the leaves in the glen where I'd found the tent, and feel the rough wood of the steps of Nell's wagon. I knew I'd never forget any of it. I knew it.

"You'd better get back to your cabin," Snow said. "Your mom and dad will be wondering where you are."

"No," I said. "That's the beauty of this place, isn't it? They know I'm safe, and so do I."

Something weird happened then, or at least it felt weird at the time. Snow laughed. It was a good, strong, hearty laugh, because she didn't know any other way. It hurt my feelings, because I'd meant everything I'd said. I backed away from her on the bench we'd been sharing. She finished her laugh anyway.

"Oh, Molly," she finally said, "you are a wonder. You want to have it both ways, don't you? Adventure and surprises in the dark, but nothing to worry about, really. You are blessed."

"Because I didn't get hurt or lost?"

"Because you don't think you can," Snow said.

"Maybe I'll take Kip with me next time," I said.

I wouldn't have. I'd have run away from her if she'd asked. I don't know why I said I'd do it, unless it was to shock Snow. But Snow wasn't shocked.

"You couldn't," she said.

"Because she wouldn't go? You think she'd be afraid? You don't know Kip."

"Because she's still a little girl. Because it hasn't occurred to her yet that she'll grow up."

I might have told Snow that I'd never in my life thrown away a stuffed animal, that I slept surrounded by them, but I didn't want to make her laugh again.

She was up off the bench now, packing up the last of the things she'd take with her in her big blue canvas bag. She wouldn't wait for the rain to stop. She knew she wouldn't melt. When she spoke again, she had her back to me.

"If you go back again . . ." she said. Then she turned and looked at me. "All right. *When* you go back, you pay attention to what you're doing. The woods are as dark there as they are here, and the moon doesn't light up everything."

•   •   •

I was late for lunch, but there was plenty left. Mom had planned for us to eat on the porch — cheese sandwiches, popcorn, and ice cream for dessert, but the rain pushed us indoors. We had our picnic at the table in the kitchenette. Kip insisted she be the one who scooped the ice cream into the cones. I told her I wanted to do my own.

"Mom said I could do dessert!" she shouted.

"I wasn't here when she said that," I said. "It doesn't count for me."

"Mom said!"

"I'm doing my own."

We fought over the scoop, dripping and drizzling ice cream all over the table and the floor, which is probably what attracted the bee. It might have stayed wherever bees stay when it rains if we hadn't made such a mess.

Eventually each of us had a cone dripping with ice cream. Maybe because Kip and I had been fighting, Dad decided the time was right to kid around. He announced that he was very glad we'd called a truce and gotten the cones built, explaining, "I think ice cream tastes best when you can see the end of the summer coming, and I've been looking forward to this cone on a rainy afternoon." He opened his mouth wide, ridiculously wide, and pretended that he was about to swallow the whole scoop of ice cream. While he was making that silly face, wide-eyed and trying to make us laugh, the bee stung his tongue.

"Ouch," he tried to say, and then, "Damn." But his tongue was swelling up so fast we could hardly understand him. Then he sat down, hard, and held up one hand, as if he was trying to reassure us that he'd be all right.

For a terrible moment we watched, and then Mom shouted, "Molly! Run to the lodge and tell them to call a doctor!"

I ran. I was happy to do it. My dad was the confident, safe driver, so we could curl up happily in the back seat. He was the soccer coach who laughed at himself for getting too caught up in our games. He was the guy who'd welcomed each Father's Day card, each painted-rock paperweight, and every clay handprint we could make, year after year.

How could my dad be struggling so loudly to breathe?

Anything, anything, anything was better than watching. I ran, and I was at the front desk of the lodge in seconds, soaking wet and splashed with mud. The owner's daughter was there, Jill, home from college. I remember wishing her mother or father was at the desk, but she would have to do.

"Molly," she said, "what's —"

"My dad got stung by a bee," I said. I couldn't understand my own poise. "He can't breathe. Call —"

"Room eight," Jill said. She was pointing at the narrow stairs. "There's a doctor staying with us."

She picked up the phone. From the stairs I could hear her calm report. "Route 118. Right. Just a couple of miles beyond —"

The door to room eight opened before I could bang on it a third time. Thank goodness for the rain. Who'd have been indoors on a sunny afternoon?

"Well, hello," said the lady who opened the door.

"Are you a doctor? My dad's choking. He got stung on the tongue by a bee. We're staying —"

By then I was talking to myself, or shouting at her shadow. The doctor had opened the door in a blue cotton bathrobe with a kind of goofy smile on her face, but at my first words she'd turned back into the room in a hurry.

I heard her say, "I don't know. I'll follow her," and then, in reply to a muffled question I couldn't hear, "Yes. Make sure at the desk that they've already called for an ambulance."

"They have!" I shouted.

By then she was back, in cutoffs and a T-shirt. She was carrying a black bag. I remember wondering if all doctors carried their bags when they went on vacation, or if some of them pretended for a while that they weren't doctors.

"Show me," she said, and we crashed together down the stairs and out the front door. I heard Jill say "Oh, good," as we passed, and the doctor's husband was already on the stairs behind us.

The rain had stopped. There was mist rising off the hot ground — the pine needles and the grass — and the sun was shining through it. The air was glowing. *If it had stopped a little earlier, we'd have been outside,* I thought. *Maybe Dad wouldn't have felt like he had to make us laugh by pretending to eat his ice cream cone in one bite. Maybe the bee would have been buzzing around a flower someplace with the rest of the bees.*

"Here!" I shouted as we turned the corner and the cabin came into sight. The doctor ran past me, but not much past me. My legs were almost as long as hers.

Inside it seemed dark, but we were coming out of the sun. I saw Kip in a chair, sitting on her feet. Her eyes were wide and full of tears, but she was silent. Mom was bent over Dad, rubbing his chest, talking quietly to him. Dad wasn't choking anymore, or he didn't seem to be. He was pale. He was lying still, flat on his back, but he didn't look as if he was asleep. He looked as if somebody had knocked him out and left him there.

"I'm Pat Eberle. I'm a doctor." She already had her bag open and a needle out. "How long ago was he stung?" Now she was drawing something from a little bottle into the syringe. Now Kip started to cry.

"Maybe ten minutes," Mom said. "Maybe less. Oh, God."

"Allergies?"

"No," Mom said. "I didn't think so."

Now Dr. Eberle had Dad's shirt open and her ear on his chest. Then she was pounding on it and pushing it, pausing every few pushes to listen again. Her hands looked strong.

"Don't hurt him," Kip said. Nobody else heard her. I got up off the floor and went to her chair. I put my arms around her and turned her toward the window. I didn't want to watch, either.

But seconds after I sat down with her, Kip was up again and out of the room at a run. Mom looked up and our eyes met. Then she looked back to Dad. Nothing had changed. Dr. Eberle pounded and pushed.

Bad, I thought, *for Kip to be alone. But better for her not to see this.*

Maybe Mom was thinking the same thing.

But seconds later Kip was back, still running. She had something in her hand. Clover, it looked like, and strings of thin grass.

"Sorel," she said, "and gold thread. Snow found them in the woods. She said they were good for healing."

Dr. Eberle, God bless her, turned for a split second and took what was in Kip's hand.

Mom rode in the ambulance with Dad and Dr. Eberle. By the time it had arrived, Jill from the desk had come up to the cabin. She would stay with us, she said, and be there when my mother called from the hospital. I wished Snow hadn't already gone home.

Mom would have to call the desk and ask for us. That was why Jill took us down to the lodge to wait. It was the only time we ever watched television at the lodge.

I don't know how they kept our cabin available. Maybe it was a slower time than usual, but it hadn't seemed to be. I'm sure we should have been gone and some other family should have been there in our place, but there was no mention of it, and whenever Mom was gone somebody from the lodge was with us — Jill or somebody else from the desk, or Lisa, who was married to Dennis, who took care of the beach and the boats. Never Virginia.

I've wondered how they managed it lots of times since.

Always at the lodge everybody seemed busy. How had they all worked taking care of us into their routine?

We were fed when we were hungry, and we were never alone. I hadn't thought about what it would be like if one of my parents died. My life — our lives — hadn't always felt as secure and predictable as they did when Kip and I were curled up in the back seat of the car on the way to the lodge, where we knew that the third porch step would creak unless they'd fixed it, listening to a tape we'd practically memorized. We weren't always as sure of everything as we were at those times. But even after Nell had shown me the woods burning, I guess I hadn't understood that what she really meant was that everything would change. I thought that one day at home we would get a phone call and learn that there had been a fire in Vermont. We would sit around the dinner table — the four of us, of course — and discuss it. We'd be happy that nobody had been hurt. If it turned out that the lodge couldn't open up in the summer, we'd wonder what Snow would do. One of us would say it was impossible to imagine her not surrounded by kids in the playhouse, and everyone would agree. Somebody — probably Mom — would say we'd better start thinking about somewhere else we could go for two weeks, at least for one summer. Then, if Kip had set the table, I'd clear the dishes, unless she'd agreed to do it because I'd let her choose which TV program we'd watch that night . . . something I might have done if I was sure she'd pick the program I wanted to see.

When I smelled the woods burning, I just thought that

one day the woods would burn. Other kids my age might have understood. Some of them, even some of the kids I knew, might not even have needed Nell's sign to understand. One girl in my class at school had never known her father. He'd died in a traffic accident before she was born. She would have understood what it meant to smell the woods burn. Maybe when she read about a car crash or got caught in a line of cars behind a wreck, she would think about how soon they would sweep up the broken glass and tow away the crumpled cars. The grass that had been singed on the shoulder of the road would grow back, and the bent guardrail would be replaced with a shiny new section of galvanized metal. Everything would be the same, except that somebody who'd been in the accident might be gone, like her father was.

Or maybe she never thought about it at all, any more than I'd thought about what it might have meant to smell the woods burning. Maybe nobody thinks about how one minute you can be clowning around with a chocolate ice cream cone, and the next minute somebody can be beating on your chest while everybody waits for the ambulance to come. Maybe if everybody thought about that, nobody would get out of bed in the morning, let alone eat ice cream.

For some time there was no change in Dad's condition. Mom told Kip that he was sleeping, and Kip asked if it was like Sleeping Beauty, only it was the bee sting and not a bite of poisoned apple that had put him to sleep.

One night after Kip had gone to bed, I asked Mom if Dad was in a coma. She was spending a lot of the day at his side, but after the second or third day, she would come back to the cabin to sleep. I'd begun to wonder how many extra days we'd be able to stay.

Kip thought about it in a different way. On the third morning after Dad had been taken to the hospital, she said, "Tomorrow is the day Snow makes walking sticks. Do we get to make them again?"

TWELVE

I WENT BACK PARTLY BECAUSE IT WAS PRETTY AND PURELY fun. I don't remember thinking about how much Mom or Kip would worry if they suddenly woke up and realized they didn't know where I was, and then searched the game room, Snow's playhouse, and the beach without turning me up. Maybe I told myself I'd be back before anyone noticed I was gone. I don't remember feeling guilty about slipping off to the circus when my father might have been dying, being at the circus rather than at his bedside or with Kip and Mom at the other end of the telephone call somebody would have made from the hospital.

I remember instead that the woods were bright with starlight, though there was a pale ring of clouds around an undramatic moon. I remember walking down the road from the cabin in my sneakers, shorts, and T-shirt, wishing I'd worn a sweater but knowing I'd be warm at the circus. I remember reaching the lawn where the plastic cycles, wagons, and assorted balls were scattered and then standing with my back to Snow's porch, wondering which way I should go into the woods. And then I remember understanding for the first time that it didn't make any difference.

I turned and followed the path that started up the hill behind the playhouse. After a few yards I was between the waist-high bushes where Kip and I had often picked blueberries. A day earlier we'd noticed that the bushes had been picked almost clean, and I'd told Kip I thought it was because we'd never been at the lodge this late in the summer before.

"We're not supposed to be here now," she'd said, and for a moment I thought she meant in the woods. That hadn't been it. She knew as well as anyone that several days earlier we were supposed to have been curled up in the back seat of the car, making Mom and Dad promise that we'd come back to the lodge next summer.

The path was really nothing but a berry patch and a shortcut from Snow's hill to the row of older cabins slanting like tired hikers across the hill behind the lodge. I don't know why I picked it over the long trail through the woods to the lake, or the less-traveled ski trail that coiled up the hill through the heavier woods and out to the meadow, where you could rest and see the land fall away to the town and a little beyond. My dad called it the view you earned with climbing.

But I was right. Just past the blueberry bushes, almost before I'd have lost sight of the bikes and balls on the hill if I'd turned around, Toni stepped out from behind an oak tree.

I wondered if she would know about my dad, but I didn't ask her. I took her hand when she offered it. I didn't look back.

We climbed together. Over the rise where there should have been a cabin that needed painting — a cabin that would have had a dark blue Volvo station wagon parked beside it — stood a tall man in tight white pants and high black boots. His shirt was white, too, and open at the neck, with ruffles in the front. Over the shirt he wore a bright red brocade vest. His sleeves were rolled halfway to his elbows, and his forearms were tanned and powerful looking. On a chair beside him he'd carefully hung a heavy black swallow-tailed coat — the kind I'd seen only in portraits of actors or politicians from an earlier century. Even in the moonlight I could see that his face was as brown as his forearms. He wore a magnificent black mustache, and his eyes were black as well.

He didn't notice us immediately. He was intent on testing the action of a whip, which he made dance by ever so slightly twitching his right wrist. When he'd satisfied himself that the whip was in the right position, he raised his arm slowly and easily over his head, then brought his hand down quickly to about the level of his waist. The whip cracked like a rifle shot.

I jumped.

Toni giggled.

That was when the lion tamer noticed us there at the edge of the woods.

"Ladies!" he boomed, as if he'd expected both of us and we were equally worthy of his attention. "Ladies! Welcome to the center ring! At least, I assume that's what you've come to see?"

"You should get your eyes checked, Bruno," Toni said. She was still giggling a little.

The lion tamer recognized her voice, or her giggle. "Antoinette, my love," he said, "is that you? The moonlight isn't all it might be tonight."

"That, and you're too vain to wear your glasses," Toni said.

"Who's your friend?" asked Bruno.

Toni introduced us, and the lion tamer took my hand and kissed it, bowing as he did so. "*Enchanté,*" he said.

"Well, thank you," I said, and then, because I felt I should say something else, "Where are your lions?"

"A question to be asked," said Bruno. "I was wondering that myself when you came in."

"Not to worry," said Toni. "They'll come back for the show."

"They *are* well trained," Bruno said. He was beaming, happy that somebody had acknowledged it.

Toni smiled at him. "And they haven't anywhere else to go."

Bruno's grin faded. "True enough," he said quietly, and then, more quietly, "but perhaps not something you need mention in present company."

138

"She's smarter than you think," Toni said. "She's probably already figured it out."

I didn't know what she was talking about, but I was smart enough not to say so, at least not just then. It did strike me as strange, though, that Nell, a fortuneteller, had told me so little, and now Bruno was hinting broadly that Toni shouldn't say too much.

"Perhaps you're right," he said, stroking his magnificent mustache. "But" — he struck a pose, still as a statue, one hand raised as if in warning about something dire indeed — "perhaps not. We can never be too careful."

Toni shook her head. "Go find a lion, Bruno," she said. "Even though they'll come home, no more to roam, wagging their tails behind them, even if you don't."

"Lions don't so much wag their tails as swish them," Bruno said. "Next time you come to the show, watch and you'll see."

Then, having had the last word, he straightened his shoulders and walked, whistling, into the woods, cracking his whip along the way.

"I'll be sure to check that at the next show," Toni said. "Assuming he can find his cats. Are you hungry?"

I hadn't realized I was until she mentioned it. I nodded. At once the air was full of the wonderful smell of fried dough and the unmistakable hiss and scent of sausages and peppers on a grill.

"Where — ?" I started to ask. But then I didn't have to. Along the path in front of us there appeared a shimmering arcade of carts and booths, each strung with brightly colored lights. Here were the sizzling sausages I'd smelled and a little further on, a singing man in a red chef's cap, pulling the fried dough out of the deep fryers and sprinkling it with powdered sugar. There was pizza, too, and next a lady whose booth was crammed with large, squarish, bubbling glass containers. Side by side were orange, and red for cherry, I supposed, and blue for blueberry, rich brown for root beer, probably, and light green for lime. Pink lemonade for the timid, too. There was also cotton candy in half a dozen colors, and in the next booth two long cabinets with a dozen or more big cartons of ice cream in flavors like Chocolate Fudge Ripple, Strawberry Explosion, Green Mint Glitter, and Big Top Extravaganza, which looked like a little bit of everything . . . or, actually, a lot of everything, since the boy who was scooping the ice cream out of that carton had a generous hand.

(He had a generous sort of smile, too, and his blond hair kind of fell into his face when he leaned into the cabinet to work his scoop into the hard, bright ice cream.)

Toni nudged me as I watched him work. "He winked at you," she said.

"No way," I told her. But he might have. He might have. He looked a little like Jimmy the Monkey, only grown up a little, and about to be grown up a lot.

Toni spun away from me toward another booth on the other side of the path. When she reappeared at my side a moment later, she had two paper plates, both star-spangled.

On each there was an ear of corn. "Fresh and hot," she said. "Let's start with this."

We ate fried chicken, too, and french fries, of course, and then washed it down with first the cherry and then the lime drinks. After that, Toni ate strawberry ice cream from a cup while I went after some cotton candy that came out of a machine in stripes: red, blue, and green. We sized up each other's food and both at once said, "That looks good," so she went for cotton candy and I walked back half a dozen booths to get ice cream.

I should have been sick. At the very least I should have been too stuffed to want to walk another step on that path. The first time Dad took Kip and me to a baseball game in Boston, he'd bought us nachos, french fries, and chocolate-covered sports bars — all before the end of the third inning. He'd wanted us to have such a good time that we'd ask to come back. I'd overheard him tell Mom that he didn't want it to be a day where all he said was "No," so I took advantage of that. I felt so sick that day after all the junk we ate that I'd have happily gone home to bed. I could have read in the paper next morning about how the Red Sox had done. But I didn't say anything. Dad wanted it to be a great day.

But after all the stuff Toni and I ate, I didn't have to pretend. The chicken was crunchy and delicious, the fries thin and salty, the bubbly drinks cold and clean on my teeth. The cotton candy melted away to nothing but the taste of fruit and sugar before I could close my mouth on it, and the ice cream — both kinds I tried — was smooth and rich.

When we'd licked our fingers clean, Toni turned to me on the plastic picnic bench we'd found for a rest and asked, "Glad you came?"

"Yes," I said. And I was. Even though Dad was in the hospital, I was. Even though Mom and Kip might be looking for me, or might need me right then as I sat on the bench next to Toni, I was glad.

"Good," she said. "I'm glad you found us again."

"It was easier this time," I said. "I hardly had to walk anywhere at all."

Toni shrugged.

"But that's weird, isn't it?" I said. "You remember the first time we saw each other? All I got was a glimpse of you in the woods, and I had to go miles out of my way for that. I was lost, stumbling down paths I'd never seen, even though I thought Snow had shown us all of them. I scratched up my ankles and ruined my shoes. And about all I saw was the pink and white of your dress as you disappeared into the trees."

Toni scrunched up her nose. "Wasn't that a stupid dress?" she said. "I'm glad I don't have to wear it anymore, even though the first time I put it on" — she stood up, and flexed her long legs until she was up on her toes, and spread her arms gracefully — "I thought it was glorious."

I laughed, and Toni smiled. But she could see I didn't want to let my question go.

"I don't know why it was that way," she said. "I don't think you should worry about it so much. You found your way here, or I found you. What does it matter? Enjoy it. I don't worry about how *I* got here."

"Do you know?"

"Sure," she said.

And then I asked a question that surprised me at least as much as it surprised Toni. I hadn't known it had been there, and suddenly there it was.

"If my dad dies, is this where he'll be?"

"Your dad?"

"He's in the hospital. He's in a coma. We're waiting, but the doctors don't know whether he'll ever come out of it. Or whatever they know, they won't tell my mother much of anything. I think Mom would tell me whatever they told her. That's the only way I'd find out, because the doctors just see Kip and me as kids who don't need to know."

I don't know how much longer I'd have rattled on if Toni hadn't put her hand on my arm. "Molly," she said. "We're not dead. We just ran away."

THIRTEEN

"WHAT?"

"We ran away," Toni said.

"From what?"

"Different people ran away from different stuff," she said. "I don't know everybody's story."

"What about Bruno?" I had to start somewhere. Toni laughed. Maybe she was relieved that I hadn't asked her to tell me her own story.

"He's not much of a lion tamer, is he?" she said. "I think he sold insurance. Sorry. Sells insurance. Some of us still do what we always did. Or at least that's the way Nell explained it to me."

"I don't get it. You mean you come here the way some people go away for the weekend or something?"

Toni frowned. "No," she said, "we're here all right. We're just there, too. The way Nell put it, what could come here came on ahead, and the rest got left behind."

"So what's here is what could . . . travel? What do you think it is? Your imagination?"

"Or the part that likes fried chicken, hot buttered corn, and strawberry ice cream," Toni said. "The part that would rather crack a whip at lions than sell insurance."

"The part that loved to dance?" I pulled back. "The part that didn't like school?" I was guessing.

Toni looked down at her plate. Then off into the woods. She stretched her legs out and flexed her toes.

"I liked school all right," she said. Something in her tone warned me away.

"What about Nell?"

"She said she was a nurse," Toni said. "Sorry. Is a nurse."

"I don't know how anybody could be a nurse," I said. "I hate hospitals."

"Why?"

It was my turn to look away. "They smell funny. And everybody's always pretending to be so cheerful. I think you'd have to be crazy to want to spend all day with sick people who might not get any better. All day you'd be seeing their relatives come in and out, worried and whispering. You'd have to be crazy to choose to do that, or you'd have to learn not to care."

"Maybe that's what Nell couldn't do," Toni said. "I'll bet that's it."

"What do you mean?"

"You're not supposed to talk about there when you're here," she said. "But Nell's different. Bruno doesn't try to sell insurance to anybody at the circus. But Nell . . . I don't know. Like I said, she's different. I guess maybe because she's a fortuneteller, she can tell other stuff, too."

"She doesn't do so well at fortunes," I said. Right away I was sorry that I'd said it. I didn't want to stifle the conversation there. But it didn't stop. I'm not even sure Toni heard my smart-aleck crack.

"She told me nursing was science and following orders," Toni said. "And she told me she was good at it. But it was also watching people die. It's hoping that what you know is going to happen won't happen this time."

Toni jumped up suddenly and turned a cartwheel right there in the clearing. It was splendid. I had turned lots of cartwheels on the front lawn at home with my friends. We turned them in front of Snow's playhouse, Kip and I and the other kids, before it was time to go for lunch. But I'd never seen one as sudden and perfect as the one Toni turned in the woods that day.

It was, I guess, a way to say, "I'm alive! I'm alive! I'm strong enough to turn these right into tomorrow." But I didn't say that, or think it then, either. As if to show me the cartwheel had been no fluke, Toni paused for the briefest, balancing instant at the end of her trick, then reversed herself and came sailing back in my direction. She might have been a watch spring. She was quick without hurry, free within the shape of the moment she made with the arc of one heel and then the other. She was the sweep of her hair and the little bounce of muscle and confidence at the end of her cartwheel. And in the wake of those cartwheels, I knew that if I followed Virginia home from the lodge one day after she'd cleared her last table and scraped her last dirty dish, I'd find the heavy shadow of this acrobat sitting silently by a dirty window in the home Virginia had described.

"She can't walk much without help," Virginia had said. "She doesn't talk much, either. She stares out the window, is what she does, and nobody knows what she's thinking about, if she's thinking anything at all."

I could have asked her. I didn't. In the woods, would you have asked her? Instead I asked her to tell me more about Nell.

"Nell didn't want to be a nurse anymore," Toni said. "At least not a nurse who watched families pray for recoveries that would never happen. A nurse who listened to patients coughing in the dark and looked in on them from the corridor by the glow of the nightlight and knew there was nothing in the world she could do for them. So she ran away."

"She told you that?"

Toni nodded.

"And people don't die here?"

"Not for Nell they don't. Not like that."

"What do you mean?"

"That's why she's here. For other people it's something else. Or it might be." Toni tossed off that mystery as if it were nothing and then frowned, as if I'd asked enough questions for the time being. "Do you ever dream you're falling?" she said.

I did, and I told her so.

"But you wake up before you land."

"Right," I said. "Somebody told me once that if you dreamt all the way to the ground, you were dead." It was one of those things we'd all just known, the same way we'd all known that rabid dogs foamed at the mouth and walked sideways, and that eating mayonnaise left too long in the sun at a picnic could kill you as dead as wandering across the turnpike. But now that I thought about it, I wondered about the falling dreams. How had anybody been able to figure out that if you were still asleep when you dreamt you hit the ground, you wouldn't wake up?

"Well, you're not," Toni said.

"Not what?"

"Not dead," she said. "You're just . . . changed." She shrugged. "Or you make a change. A change of address, anyway. You come here."

I looked at her, this turner of perfect cartwheels in the woods. "And you stay there, too?"

"It's kind of like a memory," she said. Then she jumped to her feet again and asked, "What do you want to do next?"

I shook my head and stayed where I was. "I have to work this out," I told her. "Do you — does this part of you that's here now — ever go back?"

"I dream that now sometimes," she said. "And it's real the way a dream sometimes seems to be real. But I always wake up, and I smile when I do, because I'm glad to be here."

I was, too, but I wouldn't be forever. I guess that was the difference between us that day. All the glittery acrobats, winking boys, and ice cream aside, I wanted to go back. But first I had to see Nell again, and I told Toni so.

"We can do that," she said. "She's always there." She seemed relieved that I wasn't going to ask her any more about herself.

We walked together without talking. The noise of the circus seemed to be behind us, in the direction of the lake, if the direction of the lake still had anything to do with it. (I won't say I was beginning to understand the geography of the circus, because I wasn't. The moon seemed to be in the sky where it belonged, but I wouldn't have bet I could find anything else I'd learned to count on. From the first time that I followed the sign that said CIRCUS, I had always been confused about which way I was going. About all I could figure out was that the circus seemed to be where I found it, and finding it was easier than it had once been.)

This time the noise of the circus started with only the calliope I'd come to recognize. As we walked, I could hear other instruments joining in. There were the bells and whistles and clanging symbols that no circus would be without. Bass drums, too. But there were also strings — a rich, sweet hum of them, and horns, sometimes raucous and sometimes sweetly muted, that played intricate, playful melodies above the bed of violins. Sometimes I thought I heard voices, too; a kind of circus chorus, though the words, if they were words, were so indistinct that even when I concentrated I wasn't sure I was hearing voices at all. Whispers, maybe. Or it could have been the rustle of the night woods.

Toni didn't seem to notice. She was, of course, much more sure of how to get where we were going, and she walked purposefully, with no thought of what she might stumble over, or when a tree branch might cuff her or pull at her sleeve. None did. In the light of the moon that was still ringed in shadow, she knew her way or made her way. I stayed as close to her as I could. I had purpose, too, but no confidence that I'd be able to stay on my feet if I walked into something or something walked into me.

As had happened before, I lost track of time. I had no idea how much ground we'd covered or how long we'd been walking. I couldn't even have said if we'd been making a straight line or walking in a big circle. I was about to tell Toni that, when, over her shoulder, I saw Nell's little trailer.

I knew, right away, that it was abandoned. Not just empty. Empty forever. The brightly painted door was partway open, and when we got up to the steps, we could see that Nell's table was still in the center of the little room. The lace tablecloth was still in place, too, and still covered with the tools of her trade: a crystal ball this time, for some reason, cards of various kinds, and a pencil, which Toni picked up.

"Looks ordinary, doesn't it?" she said. "But Nell showed me once how it could write by itself. She sat back, and it just started scribbling away." Toni put the pencil down where she'd found it. "Of course it probably works only for her. And even when it was working for her, it didn't seem to me that it had much to say."

Like Nell's fortunes, I thought, but maybe that wasn't fair.

She hadn't told me that my father would be in a hospital bed, or that I'd be learning words like *coma, shock,* and *oxygen deprivation,* but she'd shown me that the woods would burn. She'd tried to show me that time would pass and everything would change.

"Maybe she's gone for a walk," Toni said. "You want to play cards until she gets back?"

She was kidding. Nobody could have played the cards on Nell's table but Nell. There were no clubs, diamonds, hearts, or spades on them. There were princes in bright armor, frowning. There were ladies in flowing white or ladies in shadow, and some of the cards had just designs, black or white, and one showed a skeleton riding a black horse. I didn't know what we could play, and neither did Toni.

"You want to see Jimmy?" Toni asked.

I didn't. I didn't want to see acrobats or wild animals, musicians or clowns. Maybe it was late, or maybe it was still early, but I wanted to go home.

Toni shrugged.

I left her sitting on the steps of Nell's trailer. She didn't look as if there was anywhere she had to be. I hadn't asked her which way I should go, because by then I thought I understood that it didn't matter. From anywhere around the lodge, I could find the circus. It had gotten easier each time. And it seemed that from anywhere at the circus, I could walk into the woods, then walk out at the lodge, or at least somewhere close to something I'd recognize.

But I'd forgotten that it had been getting harder to find my way back; that, in fact, the last time it was not a cabin I'd seen or Snow's playhouse or the lake, but the dancing beam of a flashlight on thorn bushes, rocks, and crooked trees. The last time I'd come home from the circus, I hadn't found my way at all. My dad had found me.

That thought and the cold knowledge that my dad wouldn't be looking for me this time hit me when I was too far from Nell's trailer to look back and see it. But I could still hear the music of the circus — the calliope that I'd heard back before I'd known the woods as anything but Snow's domain, and the horns and strings and voices as well, if they were voices. Under the pale moon, I walked with as much sense of direction as I could manage, which was almost none at all, and I didn't seem to be getting any further from that music, no matter how much darker and less familiar the woods became.

I wondered more than once if I was walking in any direction. Was the music a little louder than it had been just a moment ago? And was that because I'd been getting closer to it, or because more players had joined in? Or because they were suddenly scraping their bows and banging their keyboards and blowing away on their trumpets more energetically? I couldn't tell, any more than I could tell whether the sounds were coming from the deeper woods to my right or from beyond the little clearing that had opened up off the path to the left — a clearing as deserted as the yard where Nell's trailer stood, as undistinguished as any picked-over berry patch, and as strange to me as Africa would have been, or Bali, or Transylvania.

I stopped when I realized I'd been running. I couldn't hear the music over the sound of my breathing. Maybe I'd been imagining that I could still hear it. Maybe because I wanted to. I'd eaten at the circus now. I'd walked everywhere with Toni and shared her jokes. I'd sat with Nell and giggled at Bruno and even half-thought it might be fun to go see Jimmy the Monkey again, but I was lost and trying to find my way home. That was true. But this was, too: The circus had been just a crooked sign on a path Snow hadn't shown us. Now it was a place I knew. At the lodge, which had been comfortable from our first day there, we were without my dad. Maybe I couldn't go back.

In the dark woods, I tried to figure that out. Daylight would come. I wouldn't be eaten by bears. You don't freeze to death in the summer, even in Vermont. Somebody would find me or I'd stumble home on my own, or so I could convince myself, even with the faint music of the circus drifting through the trees again. But if I didn't *want* to be back, if I was frightened of it, maybe I'd be better off turning around, whichever way that was, and running away to the circus for real.

Who knew how many times you could do it and still find your way home, whatever home had become or was becoming?

I imagined Toni walking in the woods by herself. "We just

ran away," she'd said. I wondered if "we" meant everybody I'd seen at the circus. Was I the only tourist?

I walked as long as there was a path to follow. Sometimes I thought I could still hear the music, but mostly not. If the musicians had been trying to call me back, maybe they'd given up and gone to bed.

When I'd first mentioned the circus to Snow, she'd asked me several questions, but she hadn't asked me if the sky was the same there as it was over our heads. If she had, I'd have said it was. I'd also have thought it was a funny question. Why wouldn't the sky have been the same?

But it wasn't. I'd been keeping my eyes on the path while I walked, trying to avoid whatever might have tripped me, but when I stopped again in the woods, which were still very much the dark woods, I looked up and saw a different sky. The moon was still pale rather than bright, ringed with shadows, but the sky itself was harder and colder. I hadn't stepped through a magical door, fallen down a hole, or climbed up a beanstalk, and the woods were still woods. A step earlier I wouldn't have been surprised if Toni had peeked out from behind any tree and smiled to see me back. Except that the sky was different. Not blacker or scarier, but active somehow. Ongoing.

And then I had it. There was the promise of winter in that sky, and it was a winter I would feel and bundle up against, but one I would run into headlong as well. Kip and I would take our sleds down the hill on the golf course near our house, a ride that was better at night for the glow of the streetlights off the shiny, packed snow. She'd sing as she dragged her sled back up the hill, because she sang everywhere. We'd argue about how many more rides we could take before Mom would be mad, decide that it was already too late and she'd be mad anyway, and sail down the hill again, whooping under a black, star-studded sky, a sky that this sky in the woods was just beginning to promise.

First there would be fall, which was crunchy apples and juicy peaches that Mom would ripen in brown paper bags on the counter. It was the new clothes, too, and new, empty notebooks for school and lots of other things to buy. For years, for both Kip and me, it had been examining the lists on the glass doors of the elementary school to see who was in our classes, but now I was in the middle school. I'd left Kip behind. Still, for both of us, it was finding out what our new soccer shirts would look like, too, and who'd be coaching us.

I stopped again under the hard sky when I thought of that, because it wouldn't be Dad, would it?

Then I heard the crackle of twigs under my feet. I was walking again. And though I still didn't know where I'd come out, I knew now plainly enough that it would be somewhere recognizable, because that's what I'd decided to do. I stepped across a fallen log and noticed, through the trees up ahead, the reflection of moonlight off something big and gray. At first I was puzzled, but after few more steps closer I recognized the back wall of the old boathouse, paintless and weathered. In an hour it would be bright enough to see what Kip and Dad and I had seen the first day we'd walked to the lake at dawn through the wet grass while Mom was tossing in her bed and muttering about what kind of vacation it was when she was woken up in the dark.

I stepped around the boathouse to be sure, but I didn't have to do it. I could hear the waves lapping at the narrow beach that would later be raked and, still later, lined with adults in lounge chairs and pocked with the sandcastles of children forbidden to go in the water right after lunch.

It had been darker in the woods. Over the lake there was nothing to get in the way of the stars and the moon. I realized, standing there just short of the line where the sand began, that I'd been hearing the crackling of branches and leaves under my feet until it had become the background noise of my night. Now there was silence — or almost. Even as that thought formed, a fish I couldn't quite have seen even if I'd known where to look leapt and slapped back into the lake.

Even in the dark, it wouldn't have been ten minutes from this spot beside the boathouse to the road that ran in front of the lodge porch, where the big, white, silent rocking chairs to the right of the screen door would be covered with dew; where the bare tables waited for red and white checked tablecloths and then mugs for the tea and the hot chocolate and the coffee you could get for yourself.

I took a long look at the cool beach in the moonlight, and the water, gray, now, at the shoreline, and black out beyond the raft. I listened to the gentle thud and clunk of the paddleboats on their short ropes as they nudged the dock. I thought again about the early morning Kip and Dad and I had walked down to the beach so Mom could sleep. "Thud, clunk" went the boats, just as they had then, unless they had been quieter that morning. Unless the lake had been so clear and smooth that breaking its surface with a rock would have scattered the silent animals and jump-started the day.

I turned from the water, walked back around the gray boathouse, and started up the path to the lodge. I knew I would see nothing in the woods I didn't understand. Now it was almost light enough so that I might have met an early swimmer coming the other way in a robe and sensible sneakers, somebody who would swim lonely laps, back and forth between the dock and the float, to build, stroke by stroke, an appetite for breakfast.

I didn't meet such a person, but I might have. And she might have said, "Sorry about your dad," because she'd have known. I'd have said, "Thanks," and she'd have gone on to her solitary laps. In some incomprehensible calculation, her "sorry" might have clicked and counted. Or maybe not.

I walked up the path and didn't see anybody.

If we'd been in one of the old cabins that summer, the screen door would have creaked when I opened it, and Mom or Kip might have woken up. But the new cabins were quiet, doors and all. I slipped into the empty living room. From the couch, I picked up the book I'd been reading before I'd gone to bed the previous night, *Huckleberry Finn*. I'd found it in one of Dad's shelves at home, and packed it for Vermont after he'd shrugged at my question about it and said, "Yes, sure. Give it a try." Huck was trying to puzzle out how Tom Sawyer could find Arabs and elephants where all Huck could see was a Sunday School picnic, when Kip wandered into the room in her pajamas, dragging her blanket and rubbing her eyes.

"I woke up and you weren't there," she said sleepily. "I hate that."

"Sorry," I said. "I couldn't sleep."

"Is Mom awake? Can we go for pancakes?"

"I think she's still asleep. And it's too early, anyway."

Kip crawled into the chair opposite me, wrapped her blanket around her shoulders, and curled up to wait until breakfast time. Before I'd found my place in *Huckleberry Finn*, she was asleep again.

A little before seven, the door to Mom's bedroom opened. I heard her step down the hall — she'd be looking into the room Kip and I were sharing, and she'd be surprised, maybe, to see the empty beds. A few moments later she was leaning over me, kissing me good morning. My mother, tired-looking but lovely, too, in her cotton nightgown covered with flowers.

"Pancakes," said Kip. She didn't even open her eyes.

Mom looked at me and smiled. On the carpet between Kip and me sat my blue sneakers, wet from the walk in the woods. I wondered if Mom would notice them and ask where I'd been, but her thoughts were elsewhere.

"Pancakes today," she told Kip. "And eat plenty. It's time to go home."

"Home?" I asked. "And leave Dad?"

"No. Of course not," she said. "We'll bring him home, too. He can stay in the hospital there as easily as he can in the one up here. And when he wakes up to come home to us, he won't have so far to go."

It was the way we talked about what had happened, and what would happen next.

I'd known the time would come, of course. We weren't going to stay at the lodge forever because Dad was in the hospital, even though he still had a tube in his arm and another one in his nose. The lodge was still a lodge. Nice as everybody was, they couldn't shuffle people around in the cabins indefinitely to accommodate the family whose dad had been stung on the tongue by a bee. We'd still have to go home. I wanted it to happen and didn't, both at once.

"We'll go over to the hospital this morning and make arrangements," Mom said.

"Maybe Dad will already be awake," Kip said.

"Maybe," Mom said.

I knew that wouldn't be true. One of the nurses would have called the lodge if there had been any change.

After breakfast we drove to the hospital. I sat in the front seat next to Mom. Kip was alone in the back. We passed the same farmhouses we always passed, and the house with the long driveway and the sign that said HOMEMADE PIES out front. Dad had always asked if we wanted to stop for pie each time we passed, and of course we never did, because none of us could imagine a dessert better than what we'd see on the menu at the lodge.

Well before we reached the bridge where you turn left for the better way into town, we drove along the part of the road from which the woods and the fields fell away steeply on the left — the place where Kip always scrunched herself way over to the right-hand side of the car and said in a squeaky voice that she was afraid she'd fall out and roll down the hill.

This time she didn't say it. She just scrunched. I looked past Mom, down the hill to the trees, a few of which were beginning to go red and orange with the season. I wondered, not for the first time, what Toni and everybody else at the circus did when the nights and days got cold. Or maybe it never got cold at the circus. I wondered, looking down the long hill into the woods, if the circus was somewhere beyond or between the trees, too, or if some other circus was there, for some other wandering child to find. It was a little like looking up at the stars on a clear night and wondering whether there were woods and roads and houses on any of the planets.

"I'm going to be sick," Kip said.

"Can you open your window and hang in there?" Mom asked.

When Kip shook her head no, Mom pulled the car over to the shoulder of the road. Kip wouldn't be sick. Sometimes she just needed to slow down, even when we weren't going very fast. Mom leaned against the car with her. I stared down into the woods.

"Mom," Kip asked, "will Dad ride home with us?"

"You feeling better?"

"Yes. Will he?"

"No," she said. "He'll be in an ambulance. They'll take him to the hospital at home, and we'll meet him there."

"Unless he woke up."

"Unless he woke up. Yes."

I realized that I had begun to think of him as my father who was in a coma, rather than my father who would wake up. For Kip it was still a matter of when, rather than if. She probably half-expected him to be sitting up in bed reading the newspaper when we arrived at the hospital. It would have delighted her more than it would have surprised her, and she'd have made a run from the doorway of the room and leapt into his arms before asking any questions. I could remember what it was like to be a little kid.

We got back into the car, Kip in the front seat this time. As Mom turned us back onto the road, she asked me to remind her to pick up some Dramamine for Kip before we started home, and I said I would.

The little hospital they'd brought Dad to looked as if it had been designed to fit into the postcard images of Vermont. It was wooden and white, and the parking lot was off to the side of the building behind a row of tall pine trees. The emergency entrance was out back, indicated by a little red arrow that you might not see, even if you were looking for it. From the front it might have been a larger, more prosperous version of the lodge. There were even a couple of columns framing the main entrance, although when you stepped inside the building, there was no mistaking where you were. You could hear the soft, padded footsteps of nurses in rubber-soled shoes on the green and white linoleum floor, and there was the scent — not heavy, but never quite absent — of antiseptic soap.

My dad's room was at the end of the corridor on the second floor. Mom didn't stop at the desk, and we followed her to the elevator.

"I don't know if the doctor will be here yet," Mom said, more to herself than to us. "I hope he is."

"I want to go home, too," Kip said. I didn't know whether she was tired of the lodge and the summer and the confusion with which we'd all been struggling since the bee sting, or whether she was just uncomfortable in the hospital.

We stepped off the elevator on the second floor and turned right down the corridor. In the rooms we passed, old men and old women lay waiting to die. Some of them were alone in the half-light made by drawn shades. In other rooms there were relatives or friends seated at bedsides. In those rooms the lights were on. Some of the visitors were talking quietly to one another.

On that day when Mom and Kip and I were walking down the corridor toward my father's room, hospitals were still new to me. I looked into the rooms we passed, seeing the old women and old men lying on their backs or curled up like children in sleep, some of them alone and not knowing it, and all I was thinking was, *My dad might not get to be old.*

When we got to his room at the end of the corridor, we found a nurse leaning over him. Maybe she was adjusting the clear plastic tube that ran from his nose, or just straightening the sheets, but for just a second, I thought she was talking to him. That was weird enough, because we hadn't been talking to Dad since he'd gone into the coma. It was easy to see he wasn't hearing anybody. But what was even more weird was that the nurse's voice was familiar, though in the instant that the thought struck me, I couldn't have said who she was.

But that didn't matter, because, weirdest of all, when the nurse heard our footsteps and turned toward us, she was Nell.

I must have made a little sound of surprise in my throat, and Nell must have thought about what she'd do next, because in her eyes — and she was looking straight and unmistakably at me — there was a warning.

"Good morning," she said to my mother, as naturally as if the earth hadn't just spun out of orbit.

"Any change?" Mom asked.

"None that I've seen, but I've only just arrived," Nell said. And then, as naturally as if she'd been at a PTA meeting, she introduced herself and took my mother's hand. Mom smiled and, in turn, introduced Nell to Kip, and to me.

Manners always, I thought. Manners even during an earthquake or a tornado. Manners when your dad is unconscious in bed and the fortuneteller from the circus in the woods has turned up at his side in a nurse's uniform.

"I'm glad to meet you," I said.

Nell smiled and gave me the tiniest nod. "I was just telling your father that I'd decided to have my lunch outside on the porch today," she said. "There was winter in the air when I woke up this morning, but it's warm again now, and I want the memory of that sunshine in my bones when the season has changed for good."

About the weather, at least, she was right. Outside the window of my father's room, the sun was shining idiotically.

Mom was looking at Nell. Kip was looking at Mom. Kip spoke first. "Could he hear you?"

"Well, he didn't say so," Nell said. "But I don't let on that I can hear everything I hear, either. So maybe he did."

Kip took a step toward the bed and said tentatively, "Daddy?"

Mom put her hand on Kip's shoulder.

Nell looked at me firmly. I didn't say a thing. Tell anyone? I don't know whom I would have told, or what I'd have said.

Dad didn't move. Kip stepped back to Mom's side. Mom could focus her attention on the nurse she didn't know.

"I haven't seen you before, have I?" she asked.

"No. I'm new."

In her nurse's uniform, with her wild hair pinned back in a bun, she looked as if she belonged precisely where she was rather than seated at a scarred wooden table in a beat-up trailer deep in the woods my mother couldn't have found with dogs and a compass. Next she bent toward Kip and took her hand. For a crazy moment, nurse's uniform or not, I thought maybe she'd turn it over and tell Kip she'd find peace after a long journey, or that she saw lots of horses in her future. "Don't worry," she said. "And don't stop talking to your daddy."

"Has Dr. Keppleman been in to see him this morning?" Mom asked.

Nell let Kip's hand go. "I don't think so," she said. "But he's in the building. I saw him downstairs not twenty minutes ago."

More to herself than to Nell, Mom said, "I wonder if he's signed what he has to sign so we can take him home?"

But Nell heard, and for the first time, she looked alarmed. And then in just another moment, she didn't. "Shall I go and try to find him for you?"

"No," Mom said. "Thank you. I'm sure you have — Kip, let's you and I go and see if we can find him. Molly, will you stay here with Dad?"

She didn't wait for an answer. In the next moment she and Kip were gone. Their departure was so abrupt, Mom's behavior so un-Momlike, that I half-thought Nell — the old Nell — was somehow responsible. She answered before I could ask. She loved to do that.

"I didn't do anything," she said.

"What are you doing here?"

"I came back," she said.

"Because you wanted to?"

"I hope I haven't upset your mother," she said. "She didn't seem entirely pleased that I was talking to your dad, did she?"

"She says we're going to take him home," I said.

"So I gathered," Nell said. "I wonder how I missed that? Maybe I don't know things anymore. Here, I mean."

"Here?"

"Rather than there, yes. At the circus. Where I knew things. Anyway, can you stop her?"

I must have looked as baffled as I felt. Stop her? Stop Mom? She was Mom.

"I can't imagine I'm back just to see you pile your dad into an ambulance and drive him back home," Nell said. "There has to be more to it than that, even if I can't see what it is anymore."

"How much could you see there? You didn't say much."

"You know, I'm not sure," said Nell. "But with the old trailer in the woods and the cards and all —"

"You didn't tell me this was going to happen to my dad."

"I knew something was going to happen to you. I knew it would change you. Rush you. I was sorry to see that."

"When I came back to the circus, you were gone."

Nell nodded. "You think we passed each other, like blind hikers?" she asked.

"Now you're a nurse again," I said. Nell smiled and half-turned, as if to show off the cut of her uniform.

Toni hadn't told me much, but it was enough to give me the impression that Nell had come to hate nursing. She'd run away from it, hadn't she? Now she had returned to the job, and she was smiling about it.

"Do you know what you're doing?"

"I'm a good nurse," she said. She was meeting my question head-on, as if she'd expected it. "I was a good nurse for a long time."

I didn't doubt her, but I wondered how much good even a good nurse could do. I'd have given a lot for Kip's faith. My father's eyes were closed. Here or at home, he wasn't with us.

"You were talking to him," I said.

"Yes." She said it as if it shouldn't have surprised anyone. "You should talk to him, too."

"Why?"

"So he'll know you're here," she said. "And to give him a place to come to."

"He doesn't look as if he can hear us," I said.

"There's nothing wrong with his ears."

"What about the rest of him? What about his brain? Nell, will he wake up?"

"You can't know now," she said. "You can talk to him, though."

"I don't think I'd know what to say."

"Or you could read to him," she said. "I'll bet you're a good reader."

She was right. I was. But what made her think it would help? Dad was as motionless as a stone. He didn't react to conversation around him and wasn't responding now, and the room was still charged with my surprise as well as the sound of our voices. I felt as if I should have pinched myself to find out if I was really talking to Nell the nurse rather than Nell the fortuneteller, or Nell the mystic, who wanted me to talk to my father.

"How do you know all this? The doctor didn't tell my mother anything about talking to him. He would have told us."

Nell looked at me for a moment, as if to give me time to prepare to take in her answer. "I guess I don't know," she said. "I'm not even sure I believe it will help him. I don't know how to be sure of that. I proceed as if I believe. I guess that's it."

In the face of her assertion, I was embarrassed. I was almost ashamed. He was my dad. If anybody should have been filled with faith that he'd wake up and drive us back home, singing with us, listening with us to the familiar story tapes, talking quietly with Mom while Kip and I half-slept in the back seat — if anybody should have believed that he would wake up and that something in the sound and presence of his family would make it happen, it should have been me.

Kip had it right. On the way to the hospital, *she* was the one who'd said, "Maybe he'll be awake when we get there." Somewhere in the hospital, small by my mother's side, she was probably saying it again.

Me, I'd thought, *Fat chance.* I'd started thinking of myself as a teenager without a father. I had two friends whose fathers had died, one of cancer, the other in an automobile accident. I'd even begun to envy them those pedestrian explanations. "Cancer" or "accident" they could say when somebody blundered into a question about the absent father. What would I say? "Bee sting"? Whoever had asked would giggle, or fight hard not to. Later one friend would say to another, "Must have been some bee." They'd both get a good laugh. The ice cream made it even worse. You could die perfectly acceptably from smoking, I thought. It was stupid and selfish, given all the warnings, but you could do it, and everyone would understand. You could die because you were driving too fast on a wet road, too, or because somebody coming the other way had fallen asleep at the wheel and suddenly come hurtling over to your side of the highway, leaving you without time to blink before the crash. But to die making a silly face? To die licking ice cream? Everybody at school would wonder what flavor.

"Oh," I said, speaking out loud before I knew I was doing it, "I don't want to go home."

"I don't want you to go home," Nell said. "Not yet. I don't know how I'd work it so I could come with you. It was challenge enough working my way in here."

So we were on the same side for different reasons, hers noble, mine selfish. She just wanted to help, and I wanted to avoid humiliation. ("Do you know Molly? I was on her soccer team last spring. Over the summer, her dad died when he and a bee went after the same ice cream cone.")

Oh, God.

"Try talking to him now," Nell said.

I shrugged. I felt weird. "Hi, Dad," I said. "I miss you."
Nell and I watched him breathing quietly.

"Tell him about your day," she said.

My day? My day had been terrible. My day hadn't been swimming and hiking and tying felt strips to a walking stick. My day have been wondering what time Mom would take us to the hospital, and then coming here and seeing that Dad was still just lying there, and that nothing had changed at all.

She must have been reading my face.

"Reading might be better," Nell said.

"What if he does wake up? What will he be like?"

"He might be different, or he might not. Once I had a patient who was in a coma for a month. He'd fallen off a ladder while he was painting his garage. He probably shouldn't have been on the ladder to begin with. It had been a hot afternoon, and he was older than I am now, and what did he know about ladders and painting the garage? He worked in a bank. But he was up there painting in the heat anyway, and he slipped. Or else he got dizzy and missed a step on the way down, having decided himself that it was no day for an old fool to be painting the garage, or that the garage could stay gray and peeling for all he cared, and he was coming down. Or maybe a rung on the ladder broke and there was a lawsuit coming at the end of the story. He worked in a bank. He must have known lawyers."

She sighed. "You see how one can talk and talk? Though little enough good it's doing your father to hear *my* voice, I'm sure."

170

"What happened to him? You can't leave him on the ground in a heap next to his half-painted garage."

"No," Nell said. "He might have stayed there for a long time, though, silent and still in the afternoon heat, if he hadn't had a dog. His wife was out somewhere playing bridge. His neighbors were probably half-asleep in their air-conditioned TV rooms, watching the ball game. But his dog — a big, black Lab called Chester — was in the back-yard when he fell. Chester loped over and licked his face for a while, and when that didn't work, he began to bark. He set up such a racket that after a while a girl who was babysitting two houses down the street — a girl not much older than you are now — picked the two-year-old she was minding out of his sandbox and wandered over to see what all the barking was about. She called 911."

"And he was in a coma when you saw him? The same as my dad is now?"

"Worse," said Nell. "Or he looked worse, anyway. He'd smacked his throat on one rung of the ladder as he fell. Somehow he didn't break his neck. I don't know how. But his throat was red-raw where the ladder had hit it, and his wind-pipe had swollen almost shut while he was unconscious on the ground. He'd stopped breathing for some time, like your dad did after that bee stung his tongue. Only nobody knew how long he hadn't been breathing, because the girl who found him couldn't say how long Chester had been barking before she'd gone through the yard to see what was wrong, so, once the ambulance arrived, all the boys could do was make sure he could breathe *then*, and hope his brain hadn't been without oxygen for so long that he'd never wake up."

"But he did."

"Yes," Nell said.

"What was his name?"

"Hector," she said. "Isn't that an odd name? There was a Greek Hector who was a hero. Maybe that's why I remember it. Though I don't suppose there's anything heroic about falling off a ladder while you're painting your garage."

"Maybe he went on to do something heroic after he woke up," I said.

Nell shrugged. "I don't think so. Or at least I never heard about it if he did. He woke up one afternoon, as I said, about a month after the accident. He said, 'Jean, my throat hurts.' That's what his wife told me. But that was because of the tube to help him breathe. It's irritating. The bruising was gone by then. You couldn't even tell he'd been hurt.

"He was confused for a while, couldn't remember some things, but that cleared up within a few days. I think it was just another week, maybe a little more, until he went back to work at the bank. Everybody told him that he looked great. They asked him if he'd lost weight."

Nell was smiling. It was a story meant to make me feel better, I guess.

"Did you come back to tell me about Hector?"

"Maybe," she said. "But I don't think it's just that. I'd have been here by your dad's bed, fiddling with the tubes and talking to him, whether you'd come in today or not."

172

"But Mom says we're going to take him home."

"I don't think that can be it," Nell said. She sat on the bed at my dad's feet. "I'm sure I'm not supposed to go with you, and I can't believe it's enough that I've told you to talk to your dad, or read to him. So I don't think he's going home yet."

"You're not the one who decides." I was sure of that.

"No," she said. "The doctor decides."

"And Mom's gone to find him."

"And it won't be much of a challenge, will it?" asked Nell. "It's a small hospital. But before he gives his okay, he'll want to look at your dad's chart. See how he's been doing."

"How he's been doing?" I said. "Nothing's changed. You can see that as well as I can."

"Look at his chart."

It was hanging on a clipboard at the foot of Dad's bed. *What a funny thing*, I thought. *All the information's in a computer, I'm sure, but it's still here on a chart, too. Handwritten. By Nell.*

"That's where they take it from to begin with," she said. "So it doesn't matter whether he calls it up on a screen in his office or waltzes right in here with your mother to look at the chart. His temperature early this morning was one hundred and two and a half. Even if your mom could arrange for an ambulance today, they won't let him travel until his temp's been normal for twenty-four hours. And a temperature is a funny thing. It could easily go back up tonight or early tomorrow morning. Easily."

She'd gotten up off the corner of the bed and walked to the window. Her back was to me when she said "Easily." In the sunlight coming through the window, she took a deep breath.

"Can you go back?"

"No," she said. "I don't think so."

"If you'd stayed in the woods, you'd never have to have seen anybody die again, would you?"

"Who told you that?"

"Nobody," I said. Nobody had.

Nell turned from the window again and looked at me. "When I became a nurse, I thought I was stronger than I turned out to be. I thought I could . . . It wasn't that I was stupid. I knew people died, even if they were getting the best care. Even if they were in the hands of nurses who'd never thought about anything but being nurses. I *knew* it. Anybody who thought about it would have known it. But knowing it didn't mean accepting it, and when it happened to my patients — when my patients died — I couldn't accept it. Oh, Molly, I hated it. I'd feel like grabbing them by the shoulders. I wanted to try to shake them back to life."

She grabbed my shoulders then, and looked into my eyes. "Wake up!" she whispered fiercely. "Don't die on me! Wake up!"

"You were a good nurse," I said. "You cared."

She let go of my shoulders and smiled. "I cared, but it got to the point that I didn't want to stay with patients who were dying. I probably should have become a school nurse or something. Nobody dies of a skinned knee on the playground, and children who do die just disappear from their classrooms, don't they? They're just there one day and not there the next, and later there's a service. That must be easier."

"So you found your way to the circus."

"I was there a couple of times when I was your age," Nell said. "I found my way back."

"What about finding your way out of the woods again after you'd been there for a long time? How did you do that?"

"It might have been impossible, Molly, but I had an idea. I followed you."

"So we didn't pass each other like blind hikers?"

"No," she said.

"That's why you weren't there the last time I went looking for you."

"That's why."

"It was harder for me to find my way out the last time."

Nell nodded. "Maybe it gets harder each time."

"And easier to find your way in?"

Nell nodded again.

"Would you go back if you could?"

Nell frowned, but only for a moment. Then she was smiling over my shoulder. Mom and Kip were at the door.

"We have to stay at the lodge some more," Kip said.

She didn't look especially upset about it. I tried to look surprised.

"Dad ran a fever early this morning," Mom said. "The doctor wants to make sure he isn't sending him out of the hospital with an infection. He wants to wait another day or two."

Nell pretended to check the little plastic valve on the tube that ran into my dad's arm. Or maybe she *was* checking it. She was a nurse, after all.

FOURTEEN

SO THAT WAS HOW THE WOODS BURNED, OR HOW THE SIGNS
and indications that they would burn came to me.

In the extra days in Vermont that Nell had found for us, I
read to Dad. I just read out loud what I was reading on my
own, which was still *Huckleberry Finn*. If he was hearing me,
I didn't figure it would bother him that I was starting partway through the book, since he'd read it lots of times. And
when I got to the part where Huck decides, that day on the
raft, that, all right, he'd rather go to hell than write the
widow that letter telling her where Jim is, I think my dad
smiled a tiny bit. I wasn't looking at him, of course, but at
the book. But he smiled. Or his lip moved a little, anyway.
Or I thought it did. Unless it was his fever.

I didn't stop reading that day. Maybe I should have gone
back and read that part I thought dad had smiled at again,
but I didn't do that, either. I pushed through the book. I'd
have read even the dumb Tom Sawyer stuff at the end,

where he makes Jim behave like a fool while he's locked in a shed, supposedly waiting to be rescued, even though Tom knows Jim's already as free as him or Huck. But way before I'd gotten to that part of the book I wished Mark Twain had left out, in fact just the next day, I had an idea about what to read next.

For all the times I'd heard it, I couldn't recite it from memory. But back at the lodge that night, I looked through the shelves in the big living room. There were mysteries and bestsellers, detective stories and collections of this and that. Cookbooks, too. I figured with all those books, Yeats had to be in there somewhere, and it turned out I was right. Tucked between a Readers' Digest collection and a book of maps, I found an old, brown, leather-bound book of his poems. Yeats. "The Song of the Wandering Aengus" was there.

We were up early the next morning, but we waited until almost nine to go, because Kip was staying with Snow this time. It would be just Mom and me at the hospital. Kip might have complained about any other arrangement that left her out of anything, but Snow never stopped being special, ever, so when Mom suggested that she leave this visit to us, Kip smiled and said okay. Then she gave me two pieces of quartz she'd found on the beach and some porcupine quills that had turned up on the dirt road that ran around the lake.

"Give these to Dad," she said. "Or just leave them on his table if he still isn't awake."

"Snow's idea?" I asked her.

Kip frowned. I guess she hadn't thought of her gifts as medicine. "I found them," she said. "It's just so he'll have something to see besides all that hospital stuff."

Her gifts and the book I'd found sat between Mom and me on the car seat as we pulled away from the lodge. Down the hill, more of the trees had burst into red and gold since I'd last looked. It would have been like a postcard, except that I knew those woods, or some of them. Kip and I and every other kid who'd ever known Snow had decorated those trees with wooden boards covered with the pictures we'd painted: flowers, rocket ships, baseball players, and little brothers. We'd named the animals, and when we couldn't find them, we'd found their tracks. We'd helped clear away the brush that choked the trails sometimes, and we'd re-painted the markings on the trees that showed hikers where each winding path went: blue circles, red diamonds, and black arrows.

And of course somewhere down that hillside turning red and gold was the beginning of a path or two where you'd lose the circles, the diamonds, and the arrows and find the circus, if that's what you were going to do.

About halfway to the hospital, Mom shifted in her seat and said, "I love Kip's optimism. I love how each time we go to the hospital, she says, 'Maybe he'll be awake when we get there.'"

"Maybe he will," I said.

"Maybe. But even if he isn't — even if he doesn't wake up for weeks or months, I hope she keeps saying it." She put her hand down on the rocks between us. "And I hope she keeps bringing or sending him things. Or making him things. I hope that wherever he is, he's surrounded by special shells she's found or pictures she's drawn or medals she's won for playing soccer or swimming." There were tears in her eyes now. "Oh," she said, "I hope you both remember him."

"I will," I said. I felt old enough to be sure it was true, even though I didn't think I'd be tested then. Wasn't I almost sure that he'd smiled at that part in *Huckleberry Finn* where the reader knows Huck has saved himself, even though Huck doesn't get it? Hadn't Nell come all the way from the circus — a much, much longer journey than I'd had to make to return, I was sure — just to help? Just to encourage me to read to Dad? And hadn't I found the poem I was sure would help if anything would? I was much older than Kip, though maybe not old enough yet to know that lots of things that people work hard together to accomplish don't work out. But if I didn't know *that* on that day I was sitting in the front seat of the car with my book in my lap and the rock and the porcupine quills beside me, I did know that Nell, a nurse so good she must have been born to it, had walked into the woods and become a fortuneteller. That's how hard the things that hadn't worked out for her must have been.

But I didn't think about it as we drove along the two-lane road that would eventually dip off the long ridge across which we were traveling and take us into the parking lot beside the little hospital where Nell sat watching Dad breathe.

I thought only that it would be good if Mom would drive a little faster.

Mom let me go to Dad's room by myself, which was a surprise. She said she wanted to talk with his doctor, so she'd stop by his office at the near end of the hall before checking on Dad. But the bigger surprise, when I got to Dad's room, was no Nell. I guess if somebody'd asked me why she wasn't there I'd have said that, of course, she had other patients, but I thought of her as just sitting with Dad, especially when we weren't there.

This time she wasn't. Nothing else had changed. Dad lay still, the tubes undisturbed. The blue plastic water pitcher sat untouched on his night table, the result of routine or optimism. I put Kit's quills and rock beside the pitcher, walked around the foot of the bed, and sat down on the edge of the chair beside the window.

"Hey," I said. "Mom's looking for the doctor. She should be here soon. Kip stayed with Snow, so it's just you and me. I brought something else to read you, in case you feel like smiling again." (I was still sure that he had, though in the car on the way to the hospital, Mom had said that maybe I had *wanted* him to smile so much that I'd imagined it.)

"I didn't have any of your books up here," I said. "So it's a good thing this poem's in a lot of collections. Or at least it was in the only one I could find. There's not much poetry on the living room shelves at the lodge. I guess they figured everybody would rather read mysteries and romances on vacation."

Maybe if Dad had been awake, and if he'd known what I was about to read him, he'd have said, "It's a romance *and* a mystery, isn't it, sweetheart?" Even Kip might have said it if she'd been there. She was a real reader, even as a little kid. But I was alone with my voice, so I just turned to the page I'd marked in the brown book and started reading.

> I went out to the hazel wood,
> Because a fire was in my head,
> And cut and peeled a hazel wand,
> And hooked a berry to a thread,
> And when white moths were on the wing,
> And moth-like stars were flickering out,
> I dropped the berry in a stream
> And caught a little silver trout.
>
> When I had laid it on the floor
> I went to blow the fire a-flame,
> But something rustled on the floor,
> And someone called me by my name:
> It had become a glimmering girl
> With apple blossoms in her hair
> Who called me by my name and ran
> And faded through the brightening air.
>
> Though I am old with wandering
> Through hollow lands and hilly lands,
> I will find out where she has gone,

And kiss her lips and take her hands;
And walk among long dappled grass,
And pluck till time and times are done,
The silver apples of the moon,

I paused and thought about them. Apples of silver. Apples that would shine in the light of the full moon and astonish you with their weight if you ever did pluck them. Silver apples. Or apples that only seemed magical for a moment, when the moon struck them. They would be pleasant enough to pick in autumn, sweet and juicy and good for you, but only the same apples you'd see piled in grocery bins, unless you looked out your window on just the right bright night. A child would know which apples they were then. Kip would know. And an adult would know about it, too. Mom would know. There in that too-warm hospital room I sat and swayed between the two possibilities like Toni on the high wire, halfway to the platform she'd set out to reach.

"The golden apples of the sun," Dad said.

FIFTEEN

IT CAME OUT KIND OF CROAKY. HE HADN'T TALKED IN SO long. But he smiled when he said it, and then he pointed to the blue pitcher and asked me for water.

Later our doctor at home told us it sometimes happened that way. I could have told him Nell had already told me that, but I didn't. I was too polite.

Dad had lost weight, of course, and he set about putting it back on with ice cream after dinner most nights. He said it was rehabilitation, and that when you fell off a horse, the important thing was to get back up and ride again. The bee sting didn't even put him off cones.

We didn't get back to the lodge the next summer, though, or the summer after that, either. We spent our two-week vacations at the beach and swam in the ocean instead of the lake. I wasn't sure why that happened. At first I thought maybe Mom or Dad waited too long to call for a reservation, but it might have been simpler than that. During the first

184

summer that we didn't go back, Kip wondered why and whined a little. Then she had a great time at the ocean, learning how to ride the waves on a plastic gizmo that worked sort of like a surfboard but was easier to ride. The next thing we knew, she was announcing to all of us that lakes were for scaredy-cats and the ocean was the only place for real swimming. That and growing up put the lodge behind us, I guess.

So it was left for me to go back, and I didn't do it for another several years. By then I could go on my own. I'd had a year of college, and a summer job that hadn't worked out very well. A drive to Vermont seemed like a good idea.

You can't curl up comfortably in the back seat, though, when you're driving the car, and the way seemed longer than I'd remembered. Two or three times I missed turns, even though I had the old postcard map that we had used to find the place the first two or three times.

And a lot had changed. A half-hour east of the lodge on the road we always took, there was another inn, one that had been abandoned years before we ever started coming to Vermont. Summer after summer we drove by it and watched as it sagged and slumped. There was nobody around to bother throwing stones through the windows, but it looked no less abandoned for that. The woods had closed in on it. Seasons of leaves had blown across the long front porch. It looked as if nobody had tried to open the door in years, let alone paint it.

It was a landmark, of course. Kit and I would be restless by the time we saw it, then feel better that we had just that half-hour more to go. We'd tell each other stories about how

185

we'd fix up the battered old inn and invite all our friends
there for the best summer ever. We'd dream up curtains and
imagine green rocking chairs on a clean, white porch. We'd
trade breakfast menus that would closely resemble the ones
we'd be seeing for the next week or two at the lodge, because
whose fantasy breakfast could be any more delicious than
chocolate chip pancakes or homemade apple and walnut
muffins with hot chocolate?

At the lodge, people told stories about the abandoned
place. There had been a divorce, perhaps. Maybe the inn-
keepers had just grown old, and their children had seen no
romance in cooking and cleaning for strangers, even at Vermont mountain rates. The truth was probably some dull
combination of fatigue and taxes, but Kip and I had our own
theories. Until the night I scared her so badly that she had to
sleep on the end of Mom and Dad's bed, we used to talk
about how it was probably haunted by a wild-eyed man with
a long black beard and an ax. He wandered through empty
rooms, looking for the man who'd — I don't know — stolen
his money, poisoned his family, cheated him out of the very
land upon which the ruined inn stood. His every step made
the old boards of the wooden floor creak.

We'd grown out of the stories, and I'd grown into the solitary walks that led me to the circus in the woods. But the old
inn had remained, looking a little more forlorn each year, a
little more hopeless. So it was no wonder that when I came
upon it this time, I didn't recognize it. The inn was as we'd
sometimes imagined it could be, painted white, of course,

with dark blue shutters and a neat, white fence out front. To the side of the inn, where there had been only briars and two old apple trees past bearing anything but stunted fruit for the squirrels to fight over, there was now a parking lot of white gravel. Several cars stood there. Business was good.

That's all I noticed, and I was half a mile down the road before I let myself understand that the place about which we'd told ghost stories was no more; that any stories two children told each other about the inn now would be about croquet on the lawn, family picnics, or maybe love at first sight between two teenagers, neither of whom had wanted to go to Vermont for a week with the family.

So for almost the next half-hour, I worried. *If an old, tumbledown recollection of an inn can live,* I thought, *then the lodge could die.* Or it could change, which might be worse. The lake could be noisy with powerboats. Condos, shingled and tastefully preweathered gray, could line the ridge behind the lodge where the old cabins had sat — the cabins with the cranky screen doors, the sloping hall floors, and the clunky old bathtubs standing on improbable animal feet with curly claws.

I didn't know whether to speed up or turn around.

But I'd come that far. Except for carrying with me, as I always did, a piece of smooth and pretty white rock Kip and I both said we'd seen first at the edge of the lake when she was nine and I was twelve, and which she had said without bitterness that I could have, I wasn't superstitious. I kept driving.

And I kept remembering. I could see Snow the first time

we'd met her, when I wasn't sure coming to the lodge would be such a great vacation, and Kip, tired of the routine of day camp at home, was all protest and whining. Snow smiled and won her over without trying. It was no trick. She was just being Snow. But somehow she let me in on what she was doing for Kip with the smile she had for me. She welcomed equally the dubious child and her outraged younger sister.

The narrow road dipped into the crossroads of the town, and I slowed down. I didn't stop at the general store, though by then I'd have liked one of those big chocolate chip cookies I was sure they'd still have in a jar on the counter, and a birch beer they'd have in a cooler by the cash register. I might have climbed the wooden stairs to the store's second story, too, prolonging the anticipation of the lodge, which was just up the hill now. Upstairs I'd have found gimp, I was sure of it, and rope for the rope jewelry Snow taught everybody to make, and the fine colored thread for weaving necklaces, anklets, or bracelets.

The store is so close to the road that from the car I could read some of the notices tacked to the board next to the door — the same kind of notices that had always been there: a flyer for the place where the woman sold homemade pies off her dining room table, babysitting ads posted by teenage girls desperate for any sort of work, a tractor for sale.

Then I was past the store and turning right to climb the hill. Two hundred yards up on the left was the white wooden Congregational church where we'd gone one rainy afternoon to hear a concert advertised on one of the flyers outside the store. We'd sat — the four of us — in straight-backed wooden chairs in one of the last rows, watching the earnest members of a string quartet undertake Mozart, until Kip pulled at Dad's sleeve and asked when they were going to sing. We left as quietly as we could.

I probably shouldn't have worried. The lodge was as it had always been, or it looked that way to me when I saw it again. The row of old cabins stood along the ridge to my right. I only caught glimpses through the trees of the lake far down the hill, but the glimpses were gratifying. The sun sparkled off it. The water looked cold and blue.

Except for the first summer we'd stayed at the lodge, we'd always known which cabin we were headed for when we arrived, and we'd always driven right to it. Lots of times we'd arrived after everyone had gone to bed. We'd emptied out the car in the dark and stumbled on to the attractions of the particular cabin we'd been assigned, feeling for a light switch along a wooden wall or finding our way by moonlight. The next morning we'd wake to the new place in the old woods, and for the next week Kip and I would rate it — the view of the woods it offered, the longer walk to breakfast, the beat-up, old brown leather couch you could sink into — against the other cabins we'd occupied. Some time on that first day, when one of us thought of it and when somebody who worked at the lodge happened to be out at the little desk between the dining room and the hallway that led to the Ping-Pong table and the knock-hockey game, we'd check in.

But this time I wasn't staying. I pulled the car into the dirt and gravel parking area across the road from the lodge itself. This was where you parked if you were there only for lunch or dinner. Then you crossed the road, climbed the three wooden steps to the porch, and either sat at an empty table or — if you didn't want the sun in your eyes when you were eating — went through the screen door to a table in the dining room.

More often than not, we'd waited until mealtime to make our choice. It was always a negotiation, and the sides never changed. Kip would choose the porch, even in a storm. Bugs would keep me inside — the tiny bugs that sometimes jitter around your eyes and your ears in still weather, or flies that go for your syrup. Mom liked the dining room if there was wind. Dad just wanted everybody to make up their minds so he could eat.

I locked the car, then remembered where I was and unlocked it. It was hot in the sun, and the shade of the porch looked inviting, but when I crossed the road I walked to the left of the lodge and up the bank to the lawn in front of Snow's playhouse. It was well after noon, and normally Snow would have been long gone. But the door to the playhouse was open.

"What luck," I thought to myself as I covered the last few yards of Snow's lawn, though luck might have had nothing to do with it.

Just before I reached the steps, I heard her say, "Come in." Her voice was the same, and I relaxed to hear it.

But some things had changed. Even before my eyes had adjusted to the half-light of the playhouse, I could see that Snow's hair was whiter, and that she was heavier. If she saw that I saw it, she didn't let on. She stood up from the bench that ran along the near side of the wooden table where we'd made everything Snow could think of. I was beside her before she could take a step. We hugged each other, and she slapped my back.

"Molly," she said. "What a delight."

"Not a surprise?" I asked.

She smiled, and that, too, was unchanged. Any six-year-old arriving for the first time that morning would have let go of her mom's hand as fast as Kip had surrendered when Snow had first welcomed us.

"Sit," she said, and she sat again herself. "You're all grown up."

It didn't sound dumb when she said it. More wistful.

"I'm working on it," I said.

"You're doing great."

She'd watched over the shoulders of a thousand children who'd painted ten thousand pictures and strung half again that many beaded bracelets, and she'd left them all feeling that they'd done great. At least a few of the little kids whose cuts she'd bandaged and whose lost projects she'd found must have grown up to be jerks or worse, but in her presence that didn't seem possible. If the worst of them had come back to the playhouse once in a while, he or she would have been "doing great." That was how Snow made you feel.

"I thought you'd have left," I said.

She raised an eyebrow as if to say, *Is this the sort of grownup you're becoming? You didn't believe I'd be here?*

"I just meant because it's afternoon," I said.

"And you didn't think I'd know you were coming?"

"Uh, no."

Snow slapped her knees and stood again. "I didn't," she said. "I'm here because I'm expecting somebody else." She looked at the watch on her tanned and freckled wrist. "She's late. If she makes it, you'll be glad you picked this day to visit."

Snow walked to the doorway of the playhouse and looked out over the yard. Whoever she was expecting was nowhere in sight. In fact, nobody was in sight. Maybe all the guests were at lunch, or already down at the lake, but it looked as if Snow and I had all the world of the lodge to ourselves. There was no traffic on the road, which wasn't unusual, and there was nobody on the path that wound into the woods on the other side, either. There didn't seem to be any kids in the game room at the back of the lodge, either. If there had been, we'd have heard the faint *tock* of Ping-Pong balls or the shrill calls of "I'm next!" from where we stood. Instead we could hear the birds, and I was surprised (and a little disappointed) that Snow didn't identify them for me as they called.

She had taught us and laughed with us. Summer to summer, she had remembered our names. Until I found the circus in the woods, she and her playhouse, her hikes, and her projects were the center of my days. And after I'd found it, she listened as no other adult I knew could have listened to my delight and confusion. I knew that if I'd brought it up now, she'd have remembered Toni and Jimmy the Monkey as surely as she recalled Kip and me. When she listened, she made no distinctions. What you wanted to do that day, what you were afraid of, what you'd had for breakfast, which license plates you'd seen in the parking lot, what puzzling creatures you'd met in the woods — Snow listened carefully to all of it and dismissed nothing.

"The woods are as dark there as they are here," she'd told me. "The moon doesn't show you everything." But that was about as far as she'd go with a warning. She'd been confident about me.

I got up from the table and walked across the room, which seemed smaller than it had been when I'd crayoned in it and listened, sometimes, to the monotonous rain on its roof. I put my hand on Snow's shoulder, surprised, now that I stood close beside her, that I was a little taller than she.

"Once you told me a story about a girl who'd talked to you all night — kept you awake past dawn with her troubles — and then left without so much as a thank you. I want to thank you. I guess that's why I drove here. What a good friend you were."

"You thanked me every summer, on the last day you were here. Your mother and father stood here and made sure you did it," she said.

"Well, thank you again."

Snow wrapped me in her arms then, and said, "What a

delight it was to watch you grow up." And then, a little mischievously, "and what fun to see you being a child, too. You're welcome."

"I remember," I said.

Snow smiled. "I told you that you would," she said.

There was the sound of tires crunching the gravel of the parking lot beside the lodge, and Snow released me and stepped into the doorway of the playhouse.

"There, you see," she said. "It is a good day for you to have come back. You'll have another friend here in just a minute."

We heard the slam of the door on the car we still couldn't see. Then, as we both watched, a woman appeared at the corner of the lodge and started up the hill toward the playhouse. She wore jeans and a long-sleeved flannel shirt, though the weather was warm for it. She had on hiking boots, but she didn't look as if she was much enjoying this hike. We could hear her muttering something before she'd covered half the ground between the lodge and the playhouse.

I recognized her before she was close enough to recognize me, or maybe it was that we were still standing in the shade of the playhouse and she was blinking in the sun. I moved to go down the steps and help her up the last part of the slope — the steepest part — but Snow put a hand on my arm. A few moments later, having covered the ground on her own, Nell was before us.

"This is no country for old women," she said. "Too hilly."

"Look who we have here," Snow said.

"Yes," Nell said. "Molly. I suppose I should have called to tell you she was coming. I hope she didn't give your old heart a shock."

For a second or less, Snow looked surprised. Then for half that time she seemed a little disappointed that Nell hadn't shrieked and carried on at this reunion. But that look passed from her face almost before it was there at all, and she joined Nell's game.

"You old fraud," she said. "Then why didn't you call?"

Nell looked at Snow steadily. "I don't remember," she said. "I'm still okay with the future. With the past, not so good." Then she turned to me. "Hello, Molly," she said. "How's Kip?"

"You remember, then," I said. I didn't know that it was my business to join their kidding. It just came out. Nell laughed, so it was all right.

"I remember," she said.

"Kip's big," I told her. "Her feet are bigger than mine. She plays basketball and soccer all day. When she comes home and Mom asks her what she's been up to, she shrugs her shoulders and says, 'Nothing.'"

"But you know different," Nell said.

"I'm not home anymore," I said, "except for vacations. But she doesn't talk to me as much as she used to, either."

Nell waved her hand at my complaint as if it were smoke in the air between us. "That will pass. You'll be loving sisters again. Soon. How is your mom?"

"Loving," I said. I didn't know it was what I'd say until I said it.

"No surprise there, then," Nell said with a nod. "She's a good one. And your dad?"

"He's taken up golf," I said.

"Golf!" Nell shrieked. "Golf! We saved him for golf?"

"You didn't know?" Snow teased.

Nell didn't miss a beat. "Certainly I did," she said. "I was just being polite." She looked around Snow's little room, took in the table bare of everything but crayons and paper, and said, "Which is more than might be said of you. Haven't you something to eat?"

From somewhere Snow produced tea she'd been brewing and shortbread cookies that had probably come the day before from the lodge kitchen. With a dramatic grunt, Nell lowered herself into one of the sturdy, low chairs set around the scarred worktable. She and Snow took one side and I sat on the other, each of us with our knees poking up.

We sipped our tea and must have looked ridiculous, though Snow, at least, was accustomed to the position.

"Maybe after tea we should go for a walk in the woods," I said.

"Ha!" Nell scoffed. "I don't walk much anymore except to get somewhere I have to go. It'll be exercise enough to get up out of this chair when the time comes."

As if she hadn't heard Nell, Snow asked me quietly, "Would you be a child again if you could?"

"I'd walk in the woods," I said. "This afternoon, I'd walk in the woods."

For a long moment Nell and Snow both looked at me. Then Nell took a noisy sip of tea. When she put down her cup, she said, "You could walk or run or crawl around in there on your hands and knees, but you wouldn't find 'em."

"Would you be a child again if you could?" asked Snow. It was so much the same as the first time that it sounded like a charm.

"Where have they gone?" I asked Nell. "Where's the circus?"

"If you'd taken your dad on one of those walks you took when you were a child, he wouldn't have heard the calliope," she said, "even though he was the one who'd told you what it sounded like when he was a little boy. Even though he'd given you that. Something to listen for."

"I wouldn't hear it now?"

"You *remember* it," Nell said. Her tone was more gentle. "And you?"

"Of course," she said. Then she must have seen in my eyes the question I hadn't figured out how to ask. "I ran away," she said. "That was a kind of becoming a child again. There are all kinds of children."

"And she wouldn't be a child again if she could," said Snow.

"No," Nell agreed, though when it was time to get out of her chair, she would grunt. She would complain about her old back and scold Snow for the children's furniture, too. "I wouldn't be a child again."

I believed her, but I wanted to hear more.

"Are you still sometimes scared enough to run away?"

"Scared is part of it," Nell said. "Scared is sometimes what you feel just before you find out what you can do next."

"Were you scared to come back?"

"I followed you," she said. "I wasn't alone."

"Thank you," I said.

Nell smiled. "Molly, it happens all the time. You're welcome." She reached across the table and took my hands in hers. "You're welcome to whatever you can make of me. Thank *you*."

Much later, when the sun began to set, we carried the little chairs out to the porch in front of the playhouse. One summer, long ago, Mom and Dad had timed our visit to the lodge for the Fourth of July. We'd all sat on blankets high on the hill behind the playhouse and watched the fireworks burst over the lake. At that distance, they didn't crack and bang and make you want to hold your ears. They kind of popped. Against all that sky, they weren't so much spectacular as just pretty. But when the show was over, Kip had said they were the best fireworks ever. They were the best for the rest of us because she'd said so, and because we knew that on the next Fourth of July, wherever we were, she'd say it again. Watching the sunset, I told Snow and Nell that story. Snow laughed and said that she hoped that when Kip got her driver's license and needed a destination, she'd come back and say hello, too. Nell said she remembered that Kip was a smart kid.

It got dark so gradually that, when we could no longer see each other clearly out there on the porch, we were all surprised.

"I guess it's time to go," Snow said, but none of us moved. The first bright stars had come into the night sky.